The Heart of the Matter

The corner by the library fire was obviously one of Anna's favorite nooks. Jesse remembered the small changes Anna had wrought at Norwood. He wondered how he was going to survive the desperate loneliness of life without her.

"I had hoped you would understand, Anna. It has given me a great deal of satisfaction to see you living the sort of life to which you were born. But this is not my world!"

"I think it is you who do not understand, Jesse. I'm not trying to hold you to a way of life you dislike."

Jesse retreated. The look in Anna's eyes filled him with misgivings.

"Anna, I just want you to have the best."

Boldly, she closed the distance between them and put her arms around Jesse's neck and kissed him.

"You are the best. For almost all of my life, fortune has stood between me and happiness. Are you going to let it happen again?"

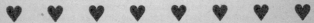

THE
GALLANT
HEIRESS

Mary E. Butler

WARNER BOOKS

A Warner Communications Company

WARNER BOOKS EDITION

Warner Books, Inc.
666 Fifth Avenue
New York, N.Y. 10103

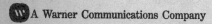 A Warner Communications Company

Printed in the United States of America

First Printing: December, 1987

10 9 8 7 6 5 4 3 2 1

prologue

The coach lurched along the icy and snow-rutted roads, sending its passengers bouncing and jolting into one another at every foot gained against the blinding storm. Wise travelers sought refuge, to wait out the storm in varying degrees of comfort, but no such thought occurred to the two women making their way so slowly along the country road. Another coachman would perhaps have been wise for them, would not have found greed more blinding than the white curtain shimmering and floating before them. Fear made an extra, uncomfortable third within the ill-sprung carriage, but his eyes looked backward rather than forward, and his voice echoed the coachman's, urging haste.

Disaster had hounded the heiress from the start of the journey. Twice it had been necessary to stop for repairs to the carriage. At the shabby hostelry where she and her chaperone had spent the night, her luggage had been ransacked while she lay in a suspiciously deep sleep. Then her chaperone, with a careless laugh, had simply deserted her. While the heiress had learned to treasure such moments of privacy, she well knew how her arrival, alone, without even a maid, would be regarded by her hostess—and her fiancé. Meeting her present companion had seemed remarkably fortuitous under the circumstances. A respectable married woman was just what she needed to lend her countenance. Also, it must be admitted, there was a forlornness and anxiety about the woman that touched the heiress's strictly controlled heart. She felt they were kindred spirits, both seeking some kind of escape.

They had spoken little since the offer of transportation had been made and accepted. Neither was of the kind to offer or invite confidences, nor were they adept at the sort of social small talk that covers such occasions.

It had been noon when they left the coaching inn in Birmingham, but already the sky was turning dark, brightened only by the increasing flurry of snow. Now an occasional flash of lightning brought the landscape into sharp focus, a frightening white sea stretching out into infinity, broken only intermittently by a stark, brilliant, ice-tipped tree. The thunderstorm, strange and out of place in winter, only served to add to the tension in the atmosphere. It frightened the horses, already slowed to a walk by the slippery road and lack of visibility.

The snow not only blinded sight, it deadened sound as well. The two horsemen were upon the travelers before they even realized their danger. One moment they were alone, isolated, in the winter storm and the next the air was full of hoarse shouts and the sound of weapons being fired. The horses, pressed already to the limit of their endurance, began to panic.

The heiress, in an unnatural state of calm, remarked, "I'm afraid they'll be terribly disappointed. I haven't so much as a timepiece to steal." An extra night on the road and the repairs to the coach had depleted her stock of ready cash considerably, but what of ransom? Quickly she pulled letters from her reticule, anything that might reveal her identity. Her substitute chaperone stared tearfully at what was probably her only possession of value—her gold wedding band.

"They shan't have it!" she swore, with more force than the heiress had thought her capable of. "What are you doing?"

The heiress was carefully feeling for a certain spot in the

carriage roof. "There's a secret panel. The thieves may check the squabs, but they won't look up here."

These few moments had been granted them as the highwaymen sought to control the fear-struck team of horses. Hardly had the women stowed away their few precious belongings when another shot rang out, no longer at random, but purposeful and directed. It was followed by a horrible cry that spoke, without any possibility of doubt, of death.

Although the women had spoken little, knew almost nothing of each other, they were now comrades, allies against the common foe. They huddled together in the corner of the coach, hands nervously clasped together for comfort.

"Good evening, ladies," a mocking voice greeted them from the open door. The cold wind rushed in, ruffling the capes of the highwayman's greatcoat about his ears. "Time for your evening constitutional. Out you go." His words were muffled by the whistling of the storm and the dark cloth that covered the lower half of his face, but the import of a swift gesture with his pistol could not be mistaken. His tawny eyes carefully looked over his prey, and although his mouth was masked, the heiress could swear that he had smiled with satisfaction.

The women stepped out timidly into a terrifying scene. A second highwayman stooped over the body of the coachman, casually searching his victim for valuables. More fearful still was the sight of the carriage team, unhitched and tied to a nearby tree with the robbers' steeds. *Of course, the horses are the most valuable booty they can take from us*, the heiress reasoned in shock, mutely protesting her fate while tacitly accepting the fact that she and her companion were intended to die.

"Your purses, ladies," the first highwayman, still maliciously polite, requested. Upon receipt of these articles from trembling fingers he tossed them to his cohort who searched them rapidly and thoroughly.

"Nothing," he proclaimed disgustedly. "Not five guineas between the two of 'em."

"Now, you wouldn't do anything so foolish as hide or try to hold back a few trinkets, would you ladies?" As the second of the robbers moved menacingly toward them, he was ordered, "Check the coach first!" The highwayman turned his tawny cat's-eyes upon his victims again. "While my friend is searching your vehicle, you might give some thought to the pure idiocy of trying to retain some gewgaws from our rapacious hands. For you shall be searched as thoroughly as that carriage until we are quite sure that there is nothing left to find."

The coach soon bore evidence of just how thorough the thieves could be. The heiress was correct, however. While the seats and squabs were dismantled and reduced to shreds, the ceiling with its concealed cache remained intact.

The thieves' failure began to produce signs of frayed nerves.

"Are you sure there's nothing hidden?" the leader of the two thieves asked.

"Search it yourself if you think you can do better."

"All right, all right. Well, ladies, this is your last chance. I won't believe these few measly pounds are all you've got. Will no one speak up?"

Perhaps both ladies realized that speech would spare them nothing, not the threatened indignities to their persons and certainly not death, for neither breathed a word.

"Tsk, tsk. Well, since you will have it so, I will be needing your cloaks and boots."

They protested, uselessly. The cloaks were ripped from their backs and torn apart, revealing nothing. With each failure the thieves' anger began to mount. Even the cynical spokesman became impatient. He did not waste time asking for their boots. A brutal shove sent each of the ladies flat in a snowdrift. The heiress looked into the dark, opaque eyes of the second, more silent, thief and thought, *He is mad; he will enjoy killing us.*

By now the highwaymen were desperate. The first pair of boots were hurled aside with a growl of rage. The chief, still holding guard with his cocked pistol, cursed aloud in disbelief. "It's got to be there!" As he moved to look for himself, his partner began to search in real earnest, moving to strip the younger and prettier of the two women, to the skin if necessary.

This proved too much for his victim. Terrified and numb from shock and cold, she suddenly became a raging wildcat. But the villain too had taken more than he could endure. He did not bother to fire his pistol. Using it as a club, he struck again and again, long past any sign of struggle.

Searching the boots, the chief had held his weapon more negligently. The older traveler too made one mad attempt at escape. From her supine position in the snow, she kicked out, upsetting the highwayman into the drift and separating him from his pistol. In a second she was on her feet and running into the storm, but the ever-deepening layer of snow pulled at her wet, frozen limbs. She was hardly a hundred feet away when a shot rang out and brought her tumbling into the snow once more. The last sound she heard as the enveloping blanket of pain and snow claimed her was the fluent cursing of the bandit for having killed too soon . . . too soon.

chapter
I

The fierce, chilling winds of the winter storm made no impact upon those foregathered in the den of the eighth Baron Norwood's sturdy country home. With curtains drawn, hearth fire ablaze, and a fine old brandy easing warmth down the throat, inclement weather could be ignored.

It was an entirely masculine gathering—one white-haired gentleman of sober years and attire; one gentleman of the genus country squire, with hair and eyes the color of ripe chestnuts, a muscular man in the prime of life; and one youth, long and gangly, but with the promise of strength and grace. At the moment the youth seemed preoccupied with keeping his brandy snifter hidden from the eyes of his elders. He sat slightly apart and silent. When addressed, he jumped, startled, and sent the forbidden brandy splashing madly.

"It's a great pity your father could not come to spend the holidays with you, Oliver," the elderly gentleman commiserated.

The eighth baron's den not only lacked the presence of any feminine influence, but it also lacked the eighth baron.

"What was it this time?" he continued. "Some political crisis, I suppose. I cannot think he has grown too timid to face a little rough weather."

"Not the weather, Doctor Abernathy. Lady Ffoulkes-Bromley," the boy answered with unrepentant impertinence. "She's buried three husbands already and now she's looking for a fourth. Papa says fighting for Whig reforms is far easier."

"My nephew, although lacking in filial respect, is not entirely mistaken in his deductions," commented the country squire. In a single graceful move, he appropriated Oliver's brandy glass and substituted one of orgeat. "Lady Ffoulkes-Bromley is a determined and experienced campaigner. Luckily for you and me, Rob, she insists on retaining her title. But no peer of the realm, unless already equipped with a spouse, is safe from her intrigues. I'm told that London hostesses must guarantee to bar her from their gates in order to assure the attendance of the most eligible bachelors."

"Norwood's usually pretty nippy in avoiding predatory females. He's certainly had enough practice all these years since Noll's mama died."

The baron's brother shrugged. It *was* a paltry excuse and Jesse Norwood had little patience with hedging about the truth. But after seven years of taking his brother's place as both estate manager and father, Mr. Norwood had learned when to keep silent.

Doctor Abernathy fumbled in his vest pocket for his snuffbox and offered a pinch to his host. "No? An old-fashioned habit, I suppose, but it suits me." He sniffed delicately and sneezed more robustly. "So Norwood won't be coming to *the wedding* then? I think Westerbrooke simply used the peerage for his invitation list. And the only people not coming are the most elderly and hidebound of Tories."

"The duke and my brother share the same politics, but nothing else. They are not upon terms—oh, in the most discreet manner. You may imagine what furor it would cause to have a public feud between two fellow Whigs and neighboring landowners. So each agrees always to invite the other to any festivities he holds, and never to accept the invitation."

"Is that so? Never would have guessed it. Over a woman,

I suppose." Doctor Abernathy, suddenly remembering the presence of young Oliver, fell into a spasm of coughs, ahemmed violently, and immediately changed the subject. "Might not have the duke speaking to me anymore if I'm not careful. Forgot and called him Lord Rowe t'other day."

"Shame on you, Rob. That's two titles ago. His father was made Viscount Gantt before he died."

The doctor chuckled. His host placed even less importance than he did on the social niceties. "The nabob was ever an ambitious man. But it seems to me if a man wants to rise in the world, there's better ways of doing it than lending money to the Prince of Wales."

"On the contrary, that's an important service to the nation," Mr. Norwood contradicted. "And I daresay a duke's coronet is a very useful thing to have—especially if you're courting an heiress." His eyes, usually a warm brown, turned cold and cynical.

"Now, Jess, you don't know that. Anyway, the wedding is certainly providing a great deal of innocent pleasure to others. You should see the village. Whole place has gone insane. Can't remember when there was such excitement before. People everywhere, the inn is packed with visitors— and they aren't even the guests!"

"You offer me a horde of strangers for entertainment? Thank you, no."

"Come, now. Aren't you the least bit curious to see the heiress? I must admit, I am. The greatest amount of money I ever saw in my entire life was a hundred pounds left to me in my grandfather's will. I would like to see a human being that is worth millions."

"You talk as if she were a specimen for your magnifying glass, or a sideshow at the fair," Mr. Norwood accused.

The doctor smiled gently. "Perhaps. It hardly seems real. My mind ceases to comprehend after the fourth zero." He circled numbers in the air.

"But, Uncle Jess, who is she? Everybody keeps talking about the heiress, but nobody calls her by name."

"True. Of course, no one has met the girl yet. The fortune is better known than the person. Well, to answer your question, the bride-to-be is the Lady Annabelle Gallant. Her grandfather was the last Marquess of Ware.''

"And he left her his whole fortune?" the boy asked.

"Yes, but there's more. Her father, Lord Merton, was a bit of an adventurer and made himself a tidy fortune in India. Then he married a princess of the Ottoman Empire, from somewhere in the Carpathian mountains, Elisabeth of Zschau, with a hefty dowry and a private collection of fabulous jewels.''

"Whew," Oliver whistled.

"Indeed. All that wealth could not help them escape from Paris once the Terror began, though. They were only just able to smuggle the child out. It was the shock of hearing of his son's death that killed the old marquess. And little Annabelle suddenly became the richest child in the world. She's been at school in the country ever since.''

"How did the duke meet her, then?"

"I don't know that he has, Noll. People like the duke commonly have arranged marriages. Almost like the alliances of princes.''

"Ugh! That sounds awful. What if she turns out to be fat and ugly? What if she's a shrew? What if they've been hiding her in the country all these years because she's mad as a Bedlamite? I saw her guardians in the village. They're ghastly! All la-di-da and tarted up. You'd think they would be a warning to the duke.''

"Presumably Westerbrooke knows what he is about. Oh, I agree with you, Noll. I would never pick a wife that way, but I wouldn't want the kind of wife—or marriage—the duke wants.''

"Be honest, Jesse," the doctor taunted. "You don't want a wife at all. This solitary existence suits you very well. Sometimes I think you actively despise the fair sex.''

"Not despise, Rob. That's too hard a word. I'll allow I've not much use for the society misses, the girls who cannot do anything for themselves, least of all think; the girls who measure a man by his title and fortune. But I don't despise them. You don't despise an ass for not being a horse; the poor thing cannot help what it is." He moved to add another log to the fire.

The doctor shook his head sadly. At thirty-seven, Jesse was too young, too ruggedly attractive still, to turn his back on romance. "All right. Name three women you admire," he challenged his friend. "Just three. I don't think you can do it."

"Yes, I can." Mr. Norwood assumed an expression of concentrated thought. The clock on the mantel ticked by a full sixty seconds.

"Come now, Jesse. Tell us before the New Year—if you can."

"The Dowager Viscountess of Sarn."

"She's ninety-two!" his nephew protested.

"I don't recall any restrictions on my choice," the gentleman answered repressively.

"One, then. Who else?"

"Mrs. Lucy."

"The housekeeper? No, I won't say another word. You've still got one more," the boy reminded him.

"Mrs. Slattery!" he finished triumphantly.

"Uncle! The carpenter's wife? She has eleven children!"

"And manages to survive. Perhaps that is why your uncle admires her," the doctor considered. "She's about to be confined again too, poor soul. I've half expected a call from one of her brood all evening. They know I'm here. Not that Maria Slattery couldn't do quite as well all by herself, except that she likes me to keep Amos calm and away from the gin."

The sounds of a door creaking and feet stamping could be heard in the hallway.

"Hullo. Is that one of them now?"

Hardly had the doctor finished his question when there was a knock on the study door. It opened to reveal a short, stocky workman to whom the aura of the stables clung irrevocably. His graying hair was also powdered with snow-flakes, which began to melt in the warmth of the room.

"Sorry to come in like this, Mr. Norwood, but I was wondering if you'd be needing any help within. I mostly knows where Lucy keeps things. Would you like me to ready a room for the doctor?"

"That won't be necessary, John," Doctor Abernathy told the groom. "I've not had so much of the brandy that I cannot get myself home all in one piece."

"Have you not seen, then?" The groom indicated the curtained windows.

Both Mr. Norwood and his nephew rose and drew back the heavy drapes to uncover an entirely different world from the one they had last seen from that spot. All familiar landmarks had disappeared, leaving only undulating plains of shimmering whiteness.

"It's beautiful," Oliver whispered.

"Yes. And dangerous," his uncle reminded him. "God pity any poor soul lost out in that tonight."

"The servants!"

"Lucy will have too much sense to try to travel back tonight. Which is why John here has so thoughtfully offered his services. It looks like we'll have to rough it for a day, probably longer." The prospect of having to fend for himself left Mr. Norwood obviously undismayed.

"That's right. All your people will be at the servants' ball at Sarn's," the doctor recalled.

"John would be there, too, but for a colicky foal."

"He's doing fine now, sir."

"That's good. The doctor can have my brother's room, since his lordship will not need it. Get a fire ready, will you, John? And take a nightshirt from my room for him."

After the groom had gone about his new duties, the doctor joined the others to stare outside at the falling snow, so light and so powerful.

"Well, it looks like I may be your guest for a while after all, Jesse."

"And very welcome you are. Although I cannot offer you the kind of hospitality I would like."

"I only hope Maria Slattery doesn't need me after all. There's not a soul could find his way through that storm and live to tell the tale."

Just at that moment the stillness of the night was broken

by a frantic pounding at the front entrance. The bell over the door jangled demandingly as the men raced to answer its summons. Oliver, the youngest and swiftest, reached the door first and nearly had it knocked out of his hands as the fierce wind pulled it open.

Swaying in the doorway was a slight figure, somehow unmistakably female even in an oversized greatcoat and men's boots. For the barest second her eyes lit up in relief. She tried to speak, but no sounds issued forth. Before Mr. Norwood could utter the words of surprise hovering on his lips, she crumpled in a heap at his feet.

chapter
II

"The deuce! Where in heaven's name did she come from?"

"Never mind where she came from," the doctor replied, "help me get her inside. If John has got the fire ready in your brother's room, we had best take her there. We've got to get her out of these wet things at once."

The lady's host scooped her up in his arms and moved swiftly up the stairs as if she were no burden at all. Doctor Abernathy disappeared momentarily and then resurfaced carrying the small black bag of his profession and a bottle of brandy.

The youth, Oliver, had raced ahead to hold open the door for his uncle. Rather than wet the bed linen, already being heated by warm bricks, Mr. Norwood brought the woman to a nearby chaise longue and tried to undo the clasp of the frozen, sodden greatcoat.

The groom, entering with a nightshirt for the doctor, halted with sudden surprise. "Merciful heavens, what's this, sir?"

"There's no time for questions now, John. If we don't get this poor woman warmed up immediately, she'll die."

"You'll want a hot bath for her then, doctor?"

"No, that would be too great a shock for her constitution. But hot bricks, all you've got. Oliver will help you."

Both the boy and the servant knew they could not afford a single moment of hesitation, could not spare a second for speculation. They must all work swiftly if a life was to be saved.

The greatcoat was peeled off with difficulty and thrown aside; the big boots were then pulled off, and the woman's stockings.

"She's like ice," Mr. Norwood whispered fearfully.

"Don't think, Jess. Just keep doing. It's the only answer," said the doctor, pouring his patient a stiff drink.

A metallic clatter announced the return of Oliver. He had cleverly used the bathtub to carry as many hot bricks and strips of flannel as possible. The boy turned around to see his uncle stripping the bodice from the pale, still form. He uttered a shocked cry.

"Don't be foolish, Noll. The lady won't thank you for excessive modesty at this time. There's no time to be lost in bashful embarrassment or adhering to the proprieties."

"But Uncle Jess—your hand!"

The moisture on Mr. Norwood's hand was not due to melted snow and ice. It shone darkly red against his skin.

"Get the rest of her clothes off and lay her down so I can see the wound," Doctor Abernathy ordered.

"It looks like a bullet wound, Rob. She's been shot in the back!"

The doctor probed and examined in silence while Oliver and the servant John continued the tiring race for more blankets and hot bricks. Hot water would have to be fetched after all, to clean the wound.

" 'Tis none so bad. In fact she's been uncommon lucky so far. The ball will have to come out, but it's not touched any vital organ. It's the cold that's the real enemy. Sometimes it goes so deep there's no way to get warm again. She's too thin as well . . ."

"She's a fighter, Rob. She wouldn't have made it this far if she gave up easily."

"Aye, she's a fighter. That can be half the battle, wanting to live."

With Jesse's help the doctor carefully cleaned the wound

and probed for the pistol ball. The lady remained unconscious throughout the operation and the bandaging of her
shoulder.

"We'll have to watch that shoulder. See that she doesn't
jostle it. Now let's get her dry and into the bed and see if we
can't get her warm."

The doctor was unable to force more than a sip of brandy
past her cold lips. The flannel nightshirt set aside for his use
was wrapped around the still form of their unknown visitor.
Carefully they transferred the lady to the great state bed in
which the barons of Norwood had been born and died for
many generations. She was then surrounded by hot bricks
wrapped in flannel and enveloped in a mountain of coverlets.

"That's all we can do for now," the doctor confessed,
"except to keep re-heating the bricks. And if she comes to
at all, try to give her some of a hot posset I'll mix up."

Oliver, curious by nature, gathered up and examined the
lady's wet garments. "A lady's shawl, bonnet, gown—
respectable, but unfashionable, clean and well-darned linen,
and a man's greatcoat and boots," he cataloged. "Hey,
Uncle Jess, there's a bullet hole in the coat!"

"Surely that's to be expected?"

"But it's in the wrong place. It's not where the lady was
shot!"

"Not? Hmmm."

"There's nothing here to say who she is. No reticule
either. Do you think she's been robbed? Although she
doesn't look like she'd have anything to steal."

"I haven't heard of any footpads or highwaymen operat-
ing in the area," the doctor said.

"Neither have I," Mr. Norwood agreed. "But with all of
London society coming this way for *the wedding* I wouldn't
be at all surprised to find a few gentlemen of the road had
decided to try their luck here."

"Surely one would have to be mad to try for a purse
tonight? The prey that type are after are too comfort-loving
to be traveling through.... Where the hell do you think
you're going?" the doctor demanded abruptly. The groom

had returned once more, this time with Mr. Norwood's outer garments.

"I'm putting on my coat. Thank you, John."

"I can see that. If you think you are going out into that storm, however, I personally will see that you are committed to Bedlam."

"Am I to leave some other poor souls out there to die and make no attempt to save them? Look at her, Rob."

Stripped of all identifying clues, the injured woman still exuded an unmistakable air of quality, one that had nothing to do with beauty or signs of indolence. Her features were too exotic for beauty, the cheekbones too pronounced, the eyes too slanted. She was not young—probably close to thirty—and had surely known hard work. Still that noble air persisted.

"She's a lady, Rob," Mr. Norwood insisted. "Oh, perhaps down on her luck, but nevertheless a lady. And a lady never travels alone. She must have come by coach. In fact, that's probably the coachman's cloak she wore. . . ."

"If so, he won't need it anymore. What you say may all be true, Jesse. But even if it were, anyone else lost in that storm must have already gone on to his Maker. This one would be dead, too, if she'd stopped for one minute and let the snow lull her to sleep. It does that, you know. You can't save them, Jess. You'll only risk your own life to no purpose. By now there won't even be any track to follow. Besides, you're needed here. We'll need to keep continuous watch, and the more her chances improve the harder time we'll have. And you've no servants but John here to keep all of us going."

It was true. "Very well," he sighed. "But it's hard to sit back and do nothing."

"Oh, you won't have time to be idle, I assure you."

Nor did he. As the night wore on he was kept on the move during his shift at the patient's bedside, continually replacing cooling bricks with hot ones and keeping the fire going briskly. Twice he thought she muttered something and he tried to give her some of the doctor's posset, but to no avail. Between the fire and the physical exertion, Mr.

Norwood was beginning to grow quite warm, even stripped to his shirt-sleeves.

As the hour approached midnight and the beginning of a new year, a change finally came, but a frightening one. The lady began to tremble from head to feet from the chill, her teeth chattering.

"Ssshh. Hush, there now." He muttered comforting words, tenderly brushing wisps of hair, fine and silky to the touch, from her forehead. "You're going to be all right. I'm here to take care of you." Her suffering tore at his heart. If only he could give his own warmth to her.

As he had once done long ago to comfort an ailing nephew, Jesse Norwood gathered the frail woman into his arms, cradling her against his chest.

Bells from the village church rang across the still night air, clear and joyous, to announce the arrival of a new year. And in the traditional master bedroom of the Barons Norwood, a mysterious lady slowly warmed to life.

chapter
III

Jesse Norwood had barely relaxed at the hopeful changes in his patient when he began to realize that she was now growing too warm and was burning up with fever.

"Aye, I was afraid of this," the doctor said when he had been fetched from his short rest. "We must still keep her warm, though, until, to put it vulgarly, we sweat it out of her. Maybe we can get her to take some of that posset now."

For two days and nights the different shifts worked to save their charge. Finally on the third night since the woman's strange and abrupt appearance, the fever broke and the doctor pronounced her out of danger.

There was a small celebration among the nurses as they heard the good news.

"Now, there's still a great deal to be done. Although the chill hasn't descended upon her lungs, for which we may thank God, she is going to wake with the grandfather of all colds. And it will be quite some time before her shoulder heals and she recovers her strength, especially as I suspect she was undernourished in the first place. She'll sleep most of the time, but she'll still need someone there with her," pronounced the doctor.

"But at least we know she'll be all right," said Oliver.

"Yes, that is a relief. I was afraid you'd expire of

frustrated curiosity if you didn't find out soon who our mysterious visitor is and where she came from,'' the boy's uncle teased, giving his hair a fond ruffle.

"But, Uncle Jess, aren't you curious to find out what happened, too?"

"Yes, boy, I am. And if the weather would only clear up, I would like to see if I can find any trace of a coach or any companions she might have had. There's the highwaymen, too, if such they were, to be caught. But all waits upon the weather."

The fierce storm of three nights ago had mellowed into a steady, consistent fall of snow. Roads remained utterly impassable. Indeed, the groom John had to fight simply to trudge to the stables and tend the horses.

"I'll be glad when the servants get back," the boy muttered as he accepted a plate of fried eggs from his uncle.

Meals were taken in the kitchen as a matter of convenience. Although Mr. Norwood had confidently said they could "rough it," the living was becoming rough indeed. None of the men had had time to shave. Only Oliver was spared an unkempt, bristly appearance simply by virtue of his youth. There was not much originality or diversity in the menus offered. Bread (increasingly stale) and cheese and eggs became the staples of their diet. A chicken was cooked to make broth, but its meat made little more than a nuncheon appetizer for the hungry men. Some attempt had been made at washing up, but housework of any other kind was ignored. The servants were likely to be warmly welcomed when they returned, and to be slightly aghast. The men, however, were far more conscious of their own hungry interiors than their exterior surroundings.

"I might take a gun out and see if there's any game to be had. . . ." Jesse's voice trailed off as he looked out the window.

"I know. As soon as the weather clears," his nephew concluded.

The patient was oblivious of all the activity around her. She slept, was fed and dosed, then slept again. Eventually, however, as the snow finally halted, so did the mysterious visitor begin to open her eyes.

At first she was a little confused, not knowing where she was, nor remembering how she came to be there. She lay in a massive bed, hung with heavy brocade curtains. These were pulled back to reveal a room handsomely furnished in an elegant, if austere, manner. In an easy chair by the hearth a boy, his fair hair falling over his brow, relaxed with a slender volume of verse. For some reason this sight seemed the strangest element of all in what must be a dream. "But why a boy?" she wondered.

She must have spoken aloud, for the youth rose, smiled, and came over to the bedside.

"You're awake! How do you do, ma'am. I am Oliver Norwood. My uncle and I are very pleased to offer you the hospitality of our home."

The voice that answered his was faint and hoarse, but cheerful and distinctly well-bred. "How do you do, Mr. Norwood. I'm sorry to be such a bother to you, and I thank you for your most gracious hospitality. My name is Anna Herries."

Even this slight effort brought on a fit of coughing, which filled the curious youth with compunction.

"Don't try to talk yet. The doctor says you must get plenty of rest. Here, let me give you some more of this tonic. I'm getting pretty good at this now." Seeing the confused look in Mrs. Herries's eyes he guessed the reason. "You're wondering why you have a clumsy idiot like me for a nursemaid. Well, I'm afraid we're quite snowed in—and the servants, having gone in a body to a special event, are snowed out. How lucky for us that the doctor was visiting. The weather is improving though, and hopefully Uncle Jesse will be able to get through to do some hunting and maybe find your coach tomorrow or the next day. It shouldn't be much longer before the roads are clear."

As memory of the terror-filled walk to the house returned, the patient's eyes grew dark and filled with tears. Her smile gone, she asked, "How long have I been here?"

"Five days now. We were quite worried when you first

came, but Doctor Abernathy says you'll be right as rain. You're quite safe here, so you mustn't worry.''

"Safe," she whispered, falling back into a restless sleep.

When next the woman called Anna Herries woke, Oliver was once again reading by the fire and a sliver of sunlight was trying to peep between the drawn curtains. The creak of the big bed as she tried to pull herself up drew the boy's attention.

"Hullo, awake again? How are you today, ma'am?"

"Much better. Oliver, isn't it?"

"Yes, ma'am. At your service. Is there anything I can do for you? Anything you need?"

As the lady felt her most urgent need to be a bath, it was not a request she felt comfortable in mentioning to a young gentleman. The boy had referred to an uncle and a doctor, but no females at all. Better not to think of how she came to be in this soft lawn shift or how her needs had been cared for these past few days.

"I'm fine, thank you."

"The sun's come out at last. Would you like to see?"

She nodded shyly. The bright sunlight caused her to blink for a moment, but once her eyes grew accustomed she leaned toward it hungrily.

"Looks pretty now, doesn't it? Uncle says he and my father used to skate on the creek when it froze, but by the time we're able to walk that far it's likely to have thawed too much."

"When I was a child, my father used to make an ice pond for me in the garden. He packed the snow down until it was hard and then poured water over it."

"What a wonderful idea! And that way Uncle Jess can't fuss about it being too dangerous. He's out looking for your coach now, by the by. When he comes back you'll meet him properly. And the doctor, too. They'll be so pleased to see you looking so much better." He looked at her hopefully. "Perhaps you feel well enough to tell us what happened. . . . But only if you're feeling quite up to it," he added hastily, seeing the stricken look upon her face.

"The coach," she whispered. "In the coach—there's a

secret panel . . . in the roof. We hid our things, valuables, in there. The thieves didn't find it."

Oliver's face swiftly changed from disappointment to a luminous glow, as one who has found the Holy Grail. "A secret compartment?"

The boy felt that he had been given a marvelous present, but the donor was less sure. After Oliver had rushed off to carry the information to his uncle, the lady was filled with guilt. There was more to be found at the site of the attack than merely a secret cache, and that was more than his young eyes should see. *I should have stopped him*, she castigated herself, *but, selfishly, all I could think of was delaying his questions. They have been kind to me. And how do I repay them?* Her fingers plucked nervously at the warm coverlet. Despite the security of the Norwood home, the care and attention lavished on her, the sense of danger remained. The nightmare of that terror-filled attack upon the coach continued to haunt her. *It isn't over. What shall I do? What can I tell them?*

Jesse Norwood was more than halfway to the highroad when his nephew finally caught up with him. His attention was caught by the impact of a cold, wet projectile on the back of his neck. Twirling around to face his opponent, Jesse answered in kind with speed and considerable expertise. The mock battle might have continued for some time had not a misplaced foot on Oliver's part given his uncle an immeasurable strategic advantage and forced the youth to concede defeat.

"Ugh! It's dripping down my neck."

"Serves you right, abominable brat. That will teach you to consider the consequences of your actions. Why are you here, neglecting your duties? It is your turn to stay with our patient, is it not?" He started on his way again, pulling a sled loaded with equipment, without waiting for the answer to his question.

"It's all right, Uncle Jess. I left her a little bell to wake up the doctor if she should need anything. But she's much better now. We talked for—oh, all of five minutes."

"Then she has stamina indeed if she attended to your ramblings for so long."

Oliver made a feint as if to throw another retaliatory snowball. "I think she's quite nice," he approved generously. "She's got a good person's smile—eyes and all. But she acts as if she were surprised to be doing it, as if she were not accustomed to it. She knows how we can make an ice pond, too."

"Does she? That certainly is a recommendation."

"And oh, Uncle, you'll never guess. She says they put all their valuables in a *secret compartment*! That's why I've come—so I can show you where it is and how to open it."

"Was she able to say anything more about how she came to be in such an unfortunate position?"

"No, not even who her companions might be. She still gets tired pretty easily. When I told her what you were doing, she told me about the coach."

"Let's hope we can find it. I'm merely making an educated guess that the likeliest place for a surprise attack is the stretch of road that goes through the North Wood—lots of cover and not a dwelling in sight."

They trudged with difficulty through the deep snow for some time, their feet crunching through the crisp frosted outer layer. After the first minor snowball skirmish, Jesse had merely plowed straight ahead with his burden and stoic determination. Oliver continued to bound about like a lamb in springtime for a while, but eventually even his youthful energy was sapped.

"Lud, it seems twice as far through the snow!"

"You think this is bad? Imagine making this walk through a blizzard so fierce you can't see your own hand before your face. And your life's blood seeping out through a hole in your shoulder. And no surety that there would be anything or anyone at the other end of your journey. Our little lady is a lot more than simply nice, Noll."

Although the gentlemen were unaware of it, all of the male residents of Norwood Hall were showing a distinctly proprietary interest in their guest. They were yet to hear the story of her past, of her recent calamity, yet she had already become unmistakably and irrevocably theirs.

The only indication that Jesse and Oliver had reached the roadway was the absence of trees for a considerable space.

"Nothing. Not a sign," said Oliver dispiritedly.

"What did you expect? There's at least three feet of snow here. And some of the drifts are higher than that."

Oliver dove into a few of the largest drifts until he had to be forcibly extricated from one by his uncle. "You don't think they took the coach with them, do you?"

"No. This is all guesswork, of course, until our visitor tells her story, but I see it as a robbery gone wrong. Somebody put up a fight and then the shooting started. The thieves got rattled, set loose the horses, and ran. They couldn't take the coach. It would have delayed them far too long and would have kept them to the highroad as well."

"I know where I'd put it then," Oliver exclaimed, getting into the spirit of the thing. "On the other side of the road, that sudden hollow, almost a ditch."

"Just what I was thinking. Here. Isn't it a good thing I brought both a shovel and an ice pick?"

They had to feel their way very carefully, aware that a single misstep might bury them under three feet of snow and ice. It was Oliver whose shovel first struck wood. Excitement gave him further energy to clear away the enveloping layers of snow patiently. The job was made a little easier by the fact that the coach had tilted over on its side.

Jesse looked nervously at his nephew as more and more snow was cleared away. He doubted very much whether the boy had given any thought to what else they were likely to find other than the secret compartment. If Oliver thought of death at all, he would still be greatly shocked by the reality of it, even if it were not violent as Jesse suspected.

Snow had filled the inside of the coach and had to be carefully removed. Jesse supervised clearing a way to the secret compartment while keeping a close eye on Oliver. His sensitive hands had discovered that the carriage was not empty. He delayed further investigation until his nephew was out of the way.

With pride Oliver showed the workings of the cache-spring and pulled out a sheaf of papers and a golden ring.

"Not much of a haul, is it? I wonder why the papers were so important. They just look like letters."

"As they are not addressed to you, I suggest you put them away. Why don't you go and find the lunch I packed for myself. Lucky thing I didn't skimp on the bread and cheese, or you'd be starving by the time we got home."

"I'm a growing boy. I need lots of nourishment. Will I be glad...."

"I know. When the roads are clear and Cook and supplies come in. Actually, we should be able to get as far as the home farm tomorrow, or at least the next day."

Suddenly he turned away from the coach and was violently ill.

"Uncle Jess! Are you all right?"

"Don't move, Noll. Don't come any closer."

"But..."

"Do as you're told."

Jesse Norwood kept his eyes carefully turned away from the body of the young woman who had traveled with Anna Herries. Overcoming his nausea, he removed the body from the carriage and laid it in the snow, covering her head with his kerchief. Returning to the abandoned vehicle, he soon found the body of the coachman. Forcing Oliver to keep his distance, Jesse loaded the two bodies on the sled gingerly, then covered and secured them.

Even though he had been spared the gruesome sight, Oliver looked a little green during the homeward journey, helping to pull the terrible burden. He asked no questions, and his uncle volunteered no answers.

chapter IV

Oliver entered the house alone. His uncle still had some business to attend to.

Almost immediately he sensed something different in the air, in his surroundings. He could not quite think what it was at first, but when he was about to drop his wet clothes in a heap on the floor, the action felt oddly uncomfortable. Jesse, entering behind him, was thus surprised to see the boy neatly hang his greatcoat and scarves on a peg.

"Uncle Jess, something feels weird in here. It even smells strange."

"You're right, Noll. It smells . . . clean."

"More than that—it smells like food, real food!"

In the kitchen they found a scene of orderly activity and delicious scents. Mrs. Herries, looking fresh if somewhat undersized in one of Lady Norwood's old gowns, was stirring the ingredients of a large pot that hung over the fire. Able assistance was being rendered by John, the groom, who stoked up the fire for her and carried two loaves of fresh-baked bread from the oven.

At the sound of Oliver's voice, she turned anxiously, looking for signs of distress in the boy's face. No, it was all right. He seemed subdued, but not stricken with horror. His uncle must have. . . . Her eyes looked past Oliver to the grim

26

face behind him and widened in surprise. Why had she assumed Mr. Norwood would be an elderly man? Here was vigor and power—and shrewdness. Anna could feel a blush spreading across her cheeks. Pray heaven they might ascribe her flushed skin to the heat of the fire.

Noting this and a militant gleam in the master's eye, the groom quickly interposed his stocky figure between the gentleman and the lady.

"Now isn't this more like it, sir? We shall eat well tonight. Miss Herries here has been supervising the work force, which is myself. A very fine officer she'd have made, sir. She directs, and I wield the spoon or the broom."

"I've no doubt you did all the heavy work once you caught her, John. But how long was it before you found her at this? Where is Doctor Abernathy? Really, ma'am." Jesse turned to the culprit without waiting for an answer. "You should not be out of bed so soon. Let me take you back upstairs. John can carry on from here."

Behind the frown, Anna saw concern and something that looked very like admiration. How foolish. She must be more tired than she had guessed.

"Oh please, if I promise to be very good and rest until dinner, may I stay downstairs with you all?"

Jesse began to understand why the groom had become her accomplice rather than send her back to bed. "Very well, ma'am. But rest you must. You won't hurry your recovery by trying to do too much too soon."

Before Anna could set foot down from her stool she was gathered up in a pair of strong arms and carried into the morning room, little used since Lady Norwood's departure. The experience of being held closely in a gentleman's arms left her in a welter of pleasurably confused sensations. She opened her mouth as if to protest then closed it, still silent. Clearly words would have no effect. And perhaps he was right. It must be the exertion that left her feeling so muzzy-headed. There was something she had meant to tell him, but she couldn't think of it right now. Too tired. Too tired to trace the errant memory of a soothing voice and warm arms about her, just like now.

When Jesse returned with a coverlet to tuck around her, Anna was already fast asleep. He smiled as he pulled the quilt over her shoulders and smoothed back the wisps of hair escaping from her chignon.

Finding the house so much improved and facing the expectation of feminine company at the dinner table, the gentlemen made some attempt to spruce up their appearances. A bath and a shave did much to make them feel more civilized. Since the occasion not only marked Mrs.— Miss?—Herries's release from the sickroom (which the doctor, after scolding the patient roundly for sneaking past him earlier, permitted), but also the first dinner observed "en suite" (rather than hastily grabbed morsels, eaten at odd moments), a festive spirit prevailed. The quality of the meal, a tasty rabbit stew, did much to enhance the feeling of well-being.

After dinner—and cleaning up, on Miss Herries's insistence—the entire company withdrew to the study. Jesse insisted once more on acting as porter.

"Truly, sir, I am not used to being treated like a fragile piece of china. I will not break, I assure you."

"I know that," Mr. Norwood admitted a little gruffly. "But you've had a hard time and deserve a little pampering. It will not hurt you to relax a bit, you know."

Oh, if he only knew what danger relaxing her guard might hold! She smiled, a noncommittal action, and quickly changed the subject.

"Mr. Norwood, when you went searching this afternoon— the boy did not see?"

"No. No, I did not let him."

"Forgive me. When I told him about the cache, I wasn't thinking properly. When I realized what I had done, I tried to catch him, but he had already left."

"Don't worry about it. That reminds me." He turned and called to the boy, who was entering the room with a tea tray and cups. "Oliver! I believe you have something for our guest."

"Oh, yes. I nearly forgot. Here you are, ma'am." Oliver set down the tray and pulled a small package from his vest pocket. "Everything that was hidden in the carriage. It worked just as you said."

The lady's eyes misted over as she gazed at the bundle in her lap. "You have all been so kind to me, opening your home to me without question, without knowing who or what I am."

Mr. Norwood looked at the sign of incipient tears with a sense of panic. He would rather face a herd of rampaging bulls, or a French invasion, than one woman crying. This must be averted at once!

"We knew you were a lady in distress, ma'am, which is more than enough for any gentleman." Jesse grinned at his nephew. "It is we who should rather thank you—for providing us with more excitement that we've seen in years."

"You jest. But you have saved my life. There are no words to express how deeply grateful I am, so I will not embarrass you by trying further. But I will never forget. Never." Miss Herries bit her bottom lip a moment, as if there were something further she wished to say if she dared. If so, the thought was decisively crushed.

"I suppose the best way of displaying my gratitude is by telling how I came to be in such a sad fix. Oliver has been very patient, but I know he is anxious to hear my story."

"Why, so are we all, ma'am. We've all tried a little deduction and now we ache to discover how close to the truth our guesses have been."

"I doubt your imagination stretched so far." She untied Oliver's handkerchief to reveal the small gold ring and the letters taken from the carriage. The ring she slipped on her finger. Looking a moment into the expectant faces she felt a moment of hesitation, then said, "The only thing of value I possess. It was my grandmother's wedding ring." The letters she handed to the doctor, as the eldest person present, and perhaps one with some authority in the matter.

"I think those letters may give the reason why the coach was beset."

"Spies! Secret documents!" Oliver guessed wildly. "On their way to Napoleon himself, I wager. They must be terribly important."

"No, I shouldn't think so. Of course, I haven't seen them either, but I should think that their importance lies in the identification of the woman who carried them."

"The other woman who traveled with you . . . ?" Mr. Norwood asked.

Miss Herries lowered her eyes.

"By heaven!" the doctor cried. "These are addressed to the heiress, Lady Annabelle Gallant!"

"You mean the coach was not held up at random? They knew the heiress would be coming at that time, in that carriage?"

"Hush, Noll. Let Miss Herries tell it from the beginning."

She clenched her hands tightly in her lap and began slowly and carefully, looking at no one.

"We only met by chance. I . . . was hurrying to an interview for a new post. It was imperative that I arrive on time lest I lose any hope for the position. But I could not hire a coach to take me any further—because of the storm that was expected. Lady Annabelle's chaperone had deserted her at the coaching inn. The idea of arriving at the home where she was to meet her future husband and his family without any female companion seemed to terrify her. At the time I thought that was the only reason for her extreme sensibility and nervous tremors. Now . . . At any rate, we fell into conversation. She thought I looked respectable, I suppose. Well, the outcome was that she offered to deliver me to my destination if I would assist her and escort her first to her fiancé, the Duke of Westerbrooke. I agreed.

"The weather was terrible, of course, but her coachman seemed very competent. He would have brought us through if. . . .

"We were almost there when these two masked men appeared out of nowhere and stopped the coach. There were shots fired. Neither of us had anything worth stealing, not even Lady Annabelle. But she thought if her identity were discovered, she would be kidnapped and held for ransom. That's why she hid the letters. I put the ring in, too.

"The highwaymen had unhitched the horses and tied them with their own mounts. It was while they were tending to the horses that we had the time to hide our things. One of the two seemed to be in charge. He had a mocking way of speech, and the strangest eyes I have ever seen, yellow like a cat's. Somewhere he must have acquired some education. He 'invited' us out of the carriage. They took our reticules, of course, and then commenced searching in earnest—our luggage, the coach, our clothes, even . . . our persons. The thieves could not believe that there was nothing to be found.''

It was as if the whole horrible scene was once again before her. Her voice faltered, sank to a husky whisper, as she continued.

"It made them furious. When the younger one began to search Annabelle . . . she couldn't take anymore, she tried to fight him. He . . . he lost control. I think he was more than a little mad. She was so pretty, so vulnerable.

"The other one was pulling my shoes off to search them. They were snug, so he put his pistol down. I had nothing to lose, so I kicked at him, and while he was off balance, I tried to make a run for it. But he must have recovered quickly. I felt this massive blow to my shoulder, and fell.

"I don't really remember the rest very clearly. I must have been unconscious for a while. I remember voices. Something about 'the bodies mustn't be found . . . we were told to bury them.' And someone else said, 'Who's going to recognize her?' Then I think I was carried into the coach.

"It was the snow that woke me. We were all three in the coach and we were buried in the snow. I took the coachman's greatcoat and boots—they were of no use to him anymore, poor soul—and started walking. And by the grace of God found you.

"That's all.''

The men had remained quite still during her recital. In truth, they were in a state of shock. Finally, Jesse Norwood spoke, quietly, "I wonder what they were looking for?"

"I don't know. I've thought and thought. I honestly don't think Lady Annabelle knew either."

"Rob, is there anything in those letters to give us a clue?"

"No. They're only about arrangements for the heiress's trip and the wedding. I must say the tone of the letters does not predispose me to think well of the lady's guardians. Terse to the point of rudeness."

Jesse caught a worried frown on Miss Herries's sober face. "You have thought of something. What is it?"

"I'm not sure at all. I'm not sure I remember those voices at the end correctly. In my mind they don't sound like the highwaymen at all, not the way I first remember them. But . . ."

"Well?"

"You realize, of course, they meant to kill us from the very first."

Mr. Norwood nodded. That aspect of her story had not escaped his notice.

"But if I heard right, they did not want any evidence found. They could not leave behind anything that would lead to the heiress's identification."

"They couldn't know she would have the letters," a pale Oliver whispered.

"We don't know that. But even if they could not, they could still be fairly sure that the heiress would have something on her that would point to her identity," his uncle contradicted.

"That may be true, Jesse," the doctor finally contributed. "And I guess I can see how the lure of so much money might lead some people to risk all for its possession, even to the point of murder. But generally it is necessary that the victim be known to be dead. What is the point of killing an heiress and hiding the fact that she is dead?"

No one had an answer for that.

chapter
V

Later that evening all the members of the snowbound household discussed what was to be done about the murders, but, like everything else, action must wait "until the roads were cleared." Since there was nothing they could do yet, they tried to keep their minds off the subject, and for the most part were successful. Neither the doctor's examination of the other victims, nor John's preparations of two long boxes, were spoken of publicly. Jesse Norwood had finally been able to reach the home farm and had come back not only with food supplies, but also with Mrs. Mattingly, the farmer's wife, and two of her daughters.

"It's not fittin' that a young lady should be alone in a bachelor household. Besides, Sophronia Lucy would never forgive me if I didn't rescue that house and all her good work from the ravages of four housebound men."

The farmer's wife was pleased to approve of Miss Herries. "A real lady, with no hoity-toity airs about her." She helped alter a few of her ladyship's old gowns so that Miss Herries no longer resembled a child playing at dress-up. Although the style was nearly a decade out of date, it was still the finest wardrobe the lady had possessed.

Mrs. Mattingly also worked at "trying to put some meat on them bones." The good country meals, combined with rest and just a little healthy exercise, began to have some effect. The patient's cheeks took on a rosy glow and her form showed promise of a distinctly feminine shape. Slowly the wound in her shoulder healed. Still the memory of the ambush left her much troubled in mind when her hosts were not by to offer distraction.

Oliver read from Scott's *Minstrelsy of the Scottish Border* while Miss Herries mended and darned. The doctor taught her to play piquet and grumbled good-naturedly when she consistently won. It was Jesse Norwood's job to search up all the old music for the pianoforte, and to head construction of the ice pond. A pair of child's skates fit well enough for Miss Herries's use. Only the doctor refrained from trying his skill on the ice, preferring to keep himself safe and whole to administer aid to the others.

Not that Anna looked as if she would need assistance. After the first few tentative steps, she took to the ice as if it were her natural element. Still Jesse kept a careful eye on her and a supporting arm around her.

"If you fall," he explained, "you might injure your shoulder again."

"But I'm perfectly steady!"

"Good, then you can hold me up."

Anna laughed. Oliver was right, Jesse thought, she didn't laugh enough.

"And if you fall, you pull me down. . . ."

"Ah, but then you have a soft, cushioned fall."

From the feel of Jesse's muscled arm around her, Anna doubted he would make such a soft cushion. The thought gave rise to a warm blush and a disturbing reminder. She must be more careful, stay hidden behind the mask. These people, this man, made it so easy to relax, to forget fear. Already she had revealed more of herself than she had shown any human soul in thirteen years. What was worse, for just a few moments, with Jesse's arm around her, she had felt like that little girl on the ice pond again, felt the same innocent pleasure Oliver showed so freely.

They avoided crashing into a happily floundering Oliver.

"You envy him?" Jesse asked.

Anna smiled wryly. Her thoughts were too obvious and this man especially saw too clearly.

"Yes. He's a very fortunate lad."

"Oliver? In worldly goods, I suppose. But you wouldn't regard that. He hasn't exactly been fortunate in his family—a father who can't face him, and a mother . . . gone."

His face was grim again when he spoke of the boy's mother. Had he loved her?

"He is fortunate to have you." Embarrassed by her forwardness, Anna concentrated on her skating. In a moment she added, "And he has a most resilient character. He is able to put sorrow behind him. I don't mean that as a weakness—he's far from unfeeling. But he doesn't allow pain to rule his life."

"And you, Miss Anna? Can you forget? Can you put sorrow behind you?"

Anna looked around at the snowdrift piling up into the horizon. "Some things should not be forgotten." She looked up into her partner's concerned eyes. "You know, Mr. Norwood, I begin to think you are a very dangerous man."

In his intense concentration upon his guest's conversation, Jesse had neglected to give his feet the proper attention. Left without direction they immediately tangled. With a loud "oof," Jesse sat abruptly on the cold ice.

"Dangerous? Only to myself."

Soon they were all on a first-name basis. Formality seemed not only out of place, but also quite ridiculous considering the circumstances of their acquaintance. A confiding youth, Oliver soon filled Anna in on all the details of life at Norwood Hall. Somehow any story, whether it was about the loss of his mother, his father's political preoccupations, or his own preparations for university, always seemed to lead back to the strengths and marvels of Uncle Jesse.

It took all of Anna's considerable resources to hide her own deep desire to learn as much as possible about Norwood Hall's enigmatic master, who was no master at all. As a younger son, Jesse had no portion, no place but what he made for himself. He might have had a career in the navy, Oliver said, but his brother had asked for help and, of course, he had answered. So Jesse had taken over all the responsibilities Lord Norwood found troublesome—his estate, his son—while the baron played at politics and parties in the city. Yet by every word and deed, Jesse Norwood showed that he thought himself among the most fortunate of men. Oh, here was a dangerous man indeed—not only to her secrets, but also to her heart. How much more dangerous it was then to subtly encourage Oliver's gossip, but she did it just the same.

Yet however much she and Oliver talked—and the conversations were often lengthy—Anna remained less than communicative about herself. Revelations came at odd moments, were almost surprised out of her, slipping from her lips by accident. Her accomplishments appeared most readily, and they were many. Anna smiled and said these skills were only what a governess needed to find a respectable position, but Oliver knew the governess at his friend's house, though an estimable woman, could not boast so many talents.

The one fact that emerged was that Anna Herries was completely alone. Her parents had died when she was young. When asked if she would like to write (pending movement of the mails, of course) to reassure anyone concerned for her well-being, the answer was very definitely "no."

"What about the woman who was going to interview you for a position?" Oliver insisted.

Anna looked surprised at such innocence. "Good heavens, Oliver, what am I to her? She probably thinks I found another position. Or decided I couldn't face life buried in the country. Any number of things could have made me change my mind. All she cares about are the applicants who did show up."

"What about the place you left?"

Anna's eyes turned bleak. "I wish I could say that I had formed such close relationships with the girls or with my employers as would guarantee their continued interest in my future, but it simply didn't happen."

When Oliver looked skeptical (how could anyone not love

her?), she explained. "It is true, some governesses become part of the family, and go on to tend the next generation. The majority live a void, however, a no-man's land. An upper servant to the family, but not accepted by the servants. It's not a way of life that encourages social intercourse." There was no self-pity in her voice, only a resigned acceptance of the way things are. "One learns to become very self-sufficient."

Anna thought the boy would let go of the problem, but Oliver's curiosity was never sated, only temporarily silenced. An hour or two later he was at it again.

"Couldn't you turn to friends of your parents, people you knew when you were a child? Even if you haven't always kept in touch, once you care for somebody you never stop, no matter what, no matter how long it's been."

"I appreciate your attempt to provide me with a background of loving friends, Oliver, but I'm afraid it just won't do. My parents moved around a great deal when I was a child. We were never in one place long enough for me to form the kind of friendships you have with your school chums and boys from the neighborhood. As for my parents' friends, most of them are dead now, claimed by the same terrible plague that killed Mama and Papa."

Finally Jesse took his nephew aside and commanded that he cease to pester their guest with annoying questions that served only to remind her of an unhappy and lonely past.

Later in the evening, Jesse joined a pensive Anna by the library window and apologized for his nephew's behavior.

"Don't. There's no need. Truly. Oliver's a good boy. A sensitive boy. And I understand. He wants his romance to be perfect. The lady he—you all—rescued from certain death ought to be a princess in disguise, or a girl running away to marry her lover at the very least. An unemployed governess simply will not do."

Jesse grinned, looking very much like his nephew. "By rights you should have been the heiress."

Anna paled visibly.

"I'm sorry. I didn't mean to remind you of that poor girl."

"It's all right."

After a short embarrassed silence, Jesse spoke again rather gruffly, a sure sign of emotion. "We would like you to know—Oliver and I—that you'll never be friendless again. If you ever need assistance, funds, a place to stay, or just a sympathetic ear to listen to your troubles, you come here to us."

Anna looked away to hide suspiciously wet eyes. If she met Jesse's warm gaze, all would be lost. There was more than one secret to hide from his eyes now, and those of the heart are the most difficult. "Thank you. You have all been so kind to me. You've given me so much more than physical well-being. I had nearly forgotten there were people like you left in the world. Caution had become second nature to me. You've reminded me that cutting myself off from people only hurts me. I won't forget."

Jesse shrugged, shuffled his feet and cleared his throat, a series of maneuvers intended to convey that he was deeply touched.

From the window a sickle-shaped moon revealed still the rolling plains of white, but the view lacked the diamond sparkle of ice. Stark, bare branches were outlined against the sky where days ago they had glittered brilliantly. Oliver's snowman, so jaunty only a short time before, had lost his contours and much of his volume. Even the ice pond had become too slushy to skate upon. The longed-for day had come.

"You won't have me on your hands much longer. The roads should be clear enough for me to get to town tomorrow."

Astonished, Jesse stared at her. In his surprise, he sounded almost a little angry. "Don't be silly. You're not going anywhere. It's far too soon after your injury. The doctor won't permit it. Neither will the magistrate, if it comes to that. You're needed as a witness. We'll never find those murderous highwaymen without your help."

"I confess that I want to see our mystery solved and justice done before I move on. I'm not at all sure, however, that it's proper for me to stay on here without a hostess. Not that it matters what people say about me, but you and Oliver have a position in the community to maintain."

"Balderdash!"

"It's not, and you know it. You think I didn't know why Mrs. Mattingly decided to move in? Besides," she added in a calmer tone, "I really must start looking for another position. The ring that was saved from the thieves constitutes the total sum of my worldly goods. You've been more than generous, but I cannot live off your generosity indefinitely."

"I don't see why not. You know, in China when you save a person's life that life belongs to you."

"Oliver warned me you were used to having your own way."

"I should have realized only a damned obstinate woman would keep on walking through that blizzard."

They tried to stare each other down. Finally with a belligerent nod, Jesse conceded. "Very well. Tomorrow when I return from town, I will bring you a respectable chaperone to act as hostess. And if you will assemble some of your needlework—the kerchiefs and doilies and such—I'll see if the village store won't buy them. I know a couple of old bid . . . that is, elderly ladies who make a little extra pocket money that way. And if you're very nice to your hostess, she may be able to help you to another post, as she is related to and orders about half the county."

After Jesse had stomped, triumphant, up the stairs, Anna remained awhile curled up in the window seat. At first she smiled to herself at such ferocious kindness. Soon, however, a few tears appeared and she began to shiver with fear. The world was about to enter their private little paradise, and to Anna Herries with it must come danger.

It was Jesse Norwood's contention that as everyone had been snowed in for more than two weeks, this first truly clear day should find everyone escaping to the village—for supplies, for the sheer sake of movement, and most importantly for news. In this he was quite correct. Almost as soon as he had deposited the doctor at his surgery, Jesse spotted a large party from the duke's mansion, easily recognizable by the splendor of their garments and the shrillness of their voices. The duke would have to be told the sad news, but he was not Jesse's first quarry.

Jesse's quarry found him first. After having stabled his team at the White Lion, Jesse ambled through the inn's coffee room, greeting friends and listening to the gossip, until a sharp jab at his vertebrae pulled him up short. His attacker was correctly identified as the dowager Lady Sarn before ever he had turned around or heard her peremptory voice.

"Hey, Jess!" Another poke. "Jesse Norwood! Come talk to me, boy." At her age of ninety-two years, men were all boys to her.

"Good morrow, my lady." Jesse gave a flourish to his bow. "And how is it with you?"

"Tolerable, tolerable. As well as can be expected after having been cooped up with my fool of a daughter-in-law for two and a half weeks. Nice to get out again."

"Indeed it is. Tell me, is Viv around?"

"Think he'd let me out on my own? Tried to put me in a private parlor! Now, how am I to hear anything in a private room? I ask you. Not that there's anything much worth gossiping about. Maria Slattery had twins. They say her husband, thinking he was seeing double, promptly took the temperance pledge. The duke's heiress hasn't shown up yet, but considering the state of the roads, that's to be expected." Being intent on her own news, the sharp-sighted old lady for once missed Jesse's reaction. "Only news worth telling is our own. That slow-top grandson of mine got engaged to Lucius Potterby's youngest."

"Viv's going to get married?"

"Finally. Took him long enough. Waits 'til he's near forty and then takes up with a chit half his age." The dowager grinned wickedly. "Just a baby, but she knows how to handle him. She'll do." This was high praise indeed. "I guess that just leaves you as the last of the determined bachelors. Be warned. Some blushing beauty may get you yet."

"If you're going to get all coy on me, I may have to find another lady to help me. I was going to invite you to come and stay with us at the Hall for a while."

Lady Sarn winked at him and gave him another poke in the ribs. "Why, Jess, that's the best offer I've had in forty years."

"To act as hostess, you reprobate. Perhaps I should ask someone more respectable. . . ."

"Oh no, you've got me curious now. I'll show up invited or not. So you've got a lady coming to visit?"

"The lady is already visiting. Hold on, it's a long story and I'd rather say it just once. Where is Viv? I really do need him."

"He should be back to check on me any minute now. But I hope you don't need him for anything serious. He was never good for much, but now that love has taken hold of him, he's downright useless. Won't anybody else do?"

"I think not. Sarn is the magistrate for this parish, is he not?"

"Yes, he is. Need a magistrate, do you? What's been going on out your way, Jess?"

"Murder. That's what has been going on."

Vivian Jeffries, Viscount Sarn, entered the coffee room at that moment. The dowager's grandson was a giant of a man, as lazy and gentle as he was large. Though his grandmother was prone to disparage him loudly and often, it was obvious to the meanest intelligence that she doted upon him. And woe unto anyone who agreed with her insults!

"Hello, Jess. Grandmama tell you the big news?"

The dowager rode over Jesse's assent and congratulations. "You've been outclassed, Viv. Jesse's got even bigger news."

Lord Sarn reacted with a raised eyebrow, prepared for some sort of jest. The expression on Jesse's face, however, quickly convinced him of the seriousness of his friend's errand. Although slow and deliberate in manner, Sarn was quick on the uptake.

"I think, Grandmama, that perhaps we had best remove

to that private parlor after all. Whatever Jesse has to tell us is not for the public ear."

"Damn you, Jess," the viscount complained when the whole story had been laid in his lap. "I've just become engaged. I've got a houseful of guests, including my fiancée and future in-laws. What I have not got is time to track down a murderer. You couldn't even leave it as a simple case of highway robbery. No, you have to bring me a deliberate case of premeditated murder."

Jesse knew his friend too well to doubt his support, despite complaint. "If you solve the mystery and bring the malefactors to justice, you'll look very heroic to Miss Potterby. Most impressive."

"Miss Potterby thinks quite well of me already, thank you."

"Oh, stop fussing, boy, and tell us what's to do," the dowager demanded, brandishing her stick.

"Formal identification of the heiress, by her guardians."

"That pair, hah! I'd love to see those mincing mannequins deal with a corpse."

"Grandmama, please! Show some decorum." To Jesse, he added, "Are you quite sure you want her to visit? She's the one that needs a keeper. To continue, the lady's guardians should also be able to direct us to the girls' school the heiress attended. And from there we should be able to discover the identity of the coachman."

"That's all very well, but what do you mean to do about catching the murderers?" Jesse asked.

"Which ones? I'm sure you've already realized the highwaymen were merely paid assassins. Our extended spell of bad weather may work in our favor. They'll have had to hole up somewhere nearby, and strangers don't generally escape notice. As for those who hired them, the thing to discover is *cui bono*, don't you think? All that lovely loot?"

"Anna—that is, Miss Herries—has the idea the murder, the fact of the heiress's death, was to be hidden."

The viscount considered the idea carefully, then shook his head. "Ten to one the money's still at the bottom of it. We will need harder proof than motive anyway. Our best chance is to find the highwaymen and have them identify the others. Find a link between them.''

"Well, you know you can count on me and my people for any help. I have to go break the news to Westerbrooke now.''

"That's a job I don't envy, even if he hadn't met the girl. I'll see you later this evening, to deliver Grandmama's things. I'd like to talk to your Miss Herries as well.''

"Of course.''

"I'm looking forward to meeting Miss Herries myself.'' Lady Sarn winked at her grandson behind her host's back.

"That poor girl," the viscount muttered to their retreating forms.

chapter VI

The viscount's pity was well-deserved. Bow Street could well have profited by studying the aged dowager's methods of interrogation, perfected over an exceptionally long career as a social power. It was rumored that after only five minutes of conversation, Lady Sarn could complete one's family tree to five generations and give a pithy character sketch of each member.

A victim who stood still, however, was her primary requirement as the grande dame could no longer chase. Standing still was what Miss Herries refused to do for as long as possible. She invented one household errand after another. When her ladyship could not be induced to take an afternoon nap, Miss Herries suddenly discovered she needed one herself. Running out of excuses, she simply hid in the stables for an hour. Dinner, however, could not be avoided. To celebrate their return, and the presence of two female guests, the servants turned a simple meal into a gala occasion. Lady Sarn turned it into an inquisition.

"I never forget a face and yours looks amazingly familiar, gel. Do I know your family?" was the dowager's opening salvo.

Anna gripped her soup spoon tightly and concentrated on keeping her voice slow and deliberate as always. "I doubt it very much, my lady. My parents did not inhabit the same exalted sphere of society as you." It seemed best to keep her answers as short as possible without appearing rude. Further elaboration would only give her ladyship a lever for more questions.

"Unusual features you've got. The tilted eyes and high cheekbones. Looks almost foreign."

Jesse, seated at Anna's left side, caught the barest hint of a dimple before she answered, with a shrug. "Once I overheard Papa joking about the likelihood of some Gypsy blood in the family, but at the time I was too young to understand what he meant."

"They say the third Countess of Ballyfurloch was barren until cured by a Gypsy charm. As her husband was near seventy, one can guess what the Gypsy's charm was." No reaction but stifled amusement from the gentlemen. Well, she'd remember where she'd seen that face before soon enough. On to the heavy artillery.

"Herries . . . Herries. Would that be the Sussex family or the Dorsetshire Herries?"

"Neither, milady. My father was the last of his family."

"Humph! And your mother?"

"Her family had taken to living on the continent. I've not heard from them in many years. Considering the disturbances caused by Napoleon, I'm not sure whether there are any left."

"Her maiden name, gel!" The viscountess was getting impatient.

"Nicholls," confessed Anna.

"Ah, the Irish family. Sad story. That would be where your black hair and blue eyes come from."

"I shouldn't think so. My mother was quite angelically fair herself. I don't believe she ever mentioned relatives in Ireland, but of course children pay so little attention to matters outside their own little world."

Lady Sarn wielded her knife fiercely, as if she wished to use it for the dissection of Miss Herries's brain.

"The boy tells me your parents died in an epidemic. What was it—cholera, typhus?"

"They never breathed a word about any danger in front of me, ma'am, just hustled me into the country. I was only twelve years old at the time." *There, now let her dare ask me what year it was,* Anna thought. *She is not so cruel as to make me admit my age—especially since she most likely thinks me past thirty.*

Anna did not realize that with regained health and the care of friends she grew younger daily.

Strain was beginning to show in Anna's eyes. In order to give her at least some relief, Jesse declined to sit in lonely state with the port bottle and followed the ladies into the drawing room that had been opened for their sole use. The ploy to distract Lady Sarn by quizzing her about the upcoming wedding was less than subtle, but the dowager had reasons of her own for accepting his lead. *Let the victim relax a little, then when she is least expecting it....*

"That is exceedingly fine needlework you've done there, miss," Lady Sarn complimented.

"Thank you, my lady. Mr. Norwood has arranged for the local draper to try to sell some of my work on consignment."

"Such fine stitches! Your English misses don't even learn the fancy work anymore. Don't have the patience for it. It's only the French convent schools that still teach it, or did before they all went mad over there."

"Oh? My mother taught me, as she was taught by her mother."

Lady Sarn "harumphed" in vexation and suspicion again, then grinned suddenly with recovered good humor. "Yes, very impressive. Few governesses can boast such talent. Jesse tells me you're quite a linguist as well."

"I have some French and Italian—opera Italian."

The inquisitor switched to the Gallic tongue to ask if Miss Herries had any knowledge of music.

"I have some proficiency on the pianoforte," Anna responded fluently in the same language. "If you would care to hear a few selections . . . ?"

"Later, perhaps. Do you draw?"

"My sketches are uninspired, but recognizable. I also

have some knowledge of the globe, ciphering, history, and literature.''

"A formidable catalog indeed. With the proper references you should have no trouble at all finding a position. Did I understand Jesse to say that your papers were saved from the thieves?''

"The papers were the property of the heiress. I have no references.'' Anna's voice had dropped lower.

"Pity. It will take some time to contact your employers. But since you are obliged to remain here until this situation is cleared up, a little delay won't matter much. Perhaps I am acquainted with these people. Who were they?''

A crooked smile crossed Anna's face, but it held more fear than amusement. She always possessed a special quality of stillness. Now it appeared clearly as an armored retreat, an attempt to place a wall between the world and her vulnerability.

"I should think that highly unlikely, my lady.''

"My dear, when you have lived as long as I have and spent as much time in society, there are very few people who count that you don't know something about.''

Seeing the pale tension in Anna's face, Jesse offered, "Perhaps Anna means her former employers were not of our class.''

"No,'' Anna whispered.

"Cits, were they? Well, that's no. . . .''

"No. No more, please. I refuse to invent lies for Lady Sarn's amusement, so that she may pull apart my falsehoods for flaws and watch me squirm to save myself. What a shabby return for all your kindness that would be! You look so shocked, Jesse. Have you not understood the import of her ladyship's questions? She finds me suspicious—no family, no references, no one in fact to speak in my behalf, to say 'yes, I know this woman. I can vouch for her, that she is respectable and hardworking.' You're quite correct, my lady. There never were any references. But I was not turned off without a character. I escaped—from people who would see me accused of any crime, however vile, simply to prevent my telling what I know of them. They would be believed, too, for they have friends, people of substance, to attest to their characters. You've only my word that I am what I say. If you feel that is not sufficient, I can quite understand.'' Anna's voice was becoming noticeably shaky now, but she allowed no other sign of distress to show. She rose from her seat, setting aside her interrupted needlework, with quiet dignity. ''Now, if you will excuse me, I will retire for the evening. Since I have no belongings to pack, I can be ready to leave whenever you choose. Lady Sarn. Mr. Norwood. Oliver.'' Anna curtseyed good night to them.

Her control held until she was safe behind the bedroom door. *Fool, how long did you think it could last,* she asked herself. But oh she had hoped to keep his kindness and that small spark of undeserved admiration. However much her heart had clamored for something rather different, something more, she would have been content to keep his friendship. The tears slipped down her face unchecked.

Anna was still sitting on the edge of the bed, weeping silently, when a scratching at the door announced a visitor.

''You decent?'' Oliver asked, already sticking his head in the door.

Anna hastily rubbed at the revealing wet streaks with the back of her hand, but not before Oliver's eagle eyes observed them.

''Tears! I thought so. Anna, how could you think we'd believe anything bad about you, no matter who said it? For heaven's sake, we've spent the last two weeks living together under the kind of circumstances that show up a person's character pretty quick.''

''Your uncle. . . .''

''Is presently giving Lady Sarn what-for for disturbing you. Gosh, you couldn't have picked a better way of raising his opinion of you than admitting your story so honestly. Valiant for Truth is Uncle Jess. Why, he can't even make himself say my mother is. . . .'' Oliver halted abruptly, embarrassed.

''Your mother?''

Oliver considered carefully, looking into Anna's eyes, red from weeping. ''Yes. I can tell you. Besides, it will help you to understand Uncle Jess. You see, my mother's not dead.''

''Not? But I thought. . . .''

''I know. That's what everyone is meant to think. She left about seven years ago. With another man, of course. Terribly humiliating for Papa, especially since Mother had always been sort of a social butterfly and she left him for a farmer from the colonies. Papa wouldn't think of a divorce, so they just put it out that she'd died. And I suppose they thought it would be easier on me. I'm not supposed to know, you see.''

''I see,'' she said, but very hesitantly.

''Uncle Jesse is about the only one who knows the truth. You notice he never actually said Mother was dead before? He can't bear the idea of lying, but he promised Papa to keep her real whereabouts secret.''

''He would never forgive a lie.''

''Lord, no, and from a . . . a friend it would just about kill him. But what I meant to say is, because of mother he . . . he's wary of females.''

''Because she left your father.''

''Oh, that I think he could understand. No, because she left me. And then, of course, thinking Papa was free, some of the females have acted pretty silly, chasing after him, because Baron Norwood is a good catch. Some of them even tried to get to Papa through Uncle Jess—and me, too. You can imagine how ghastly it's been. And none of them even saw Uncle Jess as a person, because he's a younger son and he won't get the title or the money. Well, the whole thing just left him with a bad taste in his mouth.''

''I'm not surprised. How any woman could be so foolish not to see. . . .''

Oliver smiled, satisfied. ''I knew you'd understand.''

''Yes, I do. I'm only surprised your uncle accepted me so readily. For all you know, I might be the worst sort of adventuress.''

The thought of the prim and respectable Miss Herries as an adventuress struck the boy as being riotously funny. ''I can just picture you trying to seduce government secrets from Papa! No, I'm sorry, Anna, you couldn't be an adventuress any more than you could be . . . a wealthy society miss. If you'd been like that, you wouldn't have become part of the family like this.''

"No, I suppose not. Your uncle doesn't tolerate the wealthy daughters of the aristocracy any better than he would a deceiver, does he?"

"Lord, no. Isn't it lucky you're nothing of the kind?"

Oliver left feeling immeasurably pleased with himself, having cheered up his new friend and hinted carefully how to handle his uncle and gain his affections. In her bedchamber, however, Anna continued to weep with renewed vigor. Rather than comfort, Noll's words had cut sharply at her tender heart and barely acknowledged hopes.

Jesse would never forgive a lie—nor would he forgive the truth. Of all the unhappiness Anna had known over the last years of mistreatment and lack of freedom, nothing was so terrible as the thought of Jesse's eyes turned, cold and unforgiving, away from her. And there was no escape, not if she kept her unspoken promise to a dead girl. There was a long moment when it occurred to her that the simplest and easiest solution would be to run. Stronger counsels, and the reminder of a plain gold ring, prevailed, and dawn found her once again calm and resigned to what must come.

chapter
VII

Lady Sarn, after the stern lecture received the previous evening, apologized with becoming, albeit hypocritical, grace for having disturbed Anna with a reminder of unhappy times. Her purpose, however, remained unchanged. The only difference would be in the technique. Since a direct approach would not serve, the dowager tried to encourage an atmosphere of reminiscence. She dropped names madly, hoping for an involuntary reaction. In all her ninety-two years, she had never found her powers of investigation so challenged.

Anna was not unaware of the lady's intent. Nor did she blame the older woman, for she knew her to be moved by affection for the Norwoods, not mere curiosity.

There still remained further questions to be answered. Jesse had prevented Lord Sarn from disturbing Anna last night, but the situation was too urgent to allow further delay. The cold noonday sunshine found the viscount once again at Norwood's door.

After only minor skirmishing (Jesse was inclined to be over-protective), Lord Sarn was left alone to question Miss Herries once more about the evening of the attack. Some seemingly insignificant detail, he reminded her, might come to mind again with proper urging.

Even more than clues to the murder, Sarn hoped to discover the secret of this woman who had made such an impact on his misogynist friend. Like Jesse, he was impressed by the courage and fortitude Anna had shown during the ambush. Had he not given his heart entirely to Miss Potterby, he too might have been entranced by Anna's gentle smiles, her appreciation of quiet pleasures and the sheer un-fussiness of her. Still, that air of mystery that surrounded her troubled him. It had no place in the ordinary picture of life at Norwood.

Sarn had great admiration for his grandmother's judgment and had sought her private opinion before facing Miss Herries. The dowager made no attempt to hide her misgivings.

"Oh, she may well be telling the truth, but she's not telling all of it. It could very well be that her secret has nothing at all to do with the heiress's murder. But from the look on her face when she watches Jesse, it doesn't bode well for the two of 'em."

"That's what I was afraid of."

"Dammit, I like the gel! She's got spirit. I've gone about this all wrong. I should have tried to show her I was a safe confidante. She could probably use someone to talk to, but I doubt she'll come to me now."

"Perhaps if Chloe were to try?"

"I suppose it won't hurt to try, but I hardly see her turning to a child some years her junior. She's damnably self-sufficient."

"She'd not have survived else," Sarn reminded her. "Come, now, what is troubling you?"

"Escape. She said she was escaping."

"And so?"

"So, if she is neither safe nor free here, then I'm afraid even if she cares for Jesse, he cannot hold her."

Sarn, too, was afraid. Hearing her story again, the viscount was more aware of how strongly Anna's journey savored of headlong flight. From the pallor of her cheeks and swollen eyelids it was also easy to deduce that Anna, at least, did not see a happy and romantic conclusion to her stay.

After they had gone over the details yet once more, Anna, exhausted, remarked, "I think I know where you learned your interrogation techniques, my lord."

The viscount smiled lazily. "No, no, a mere novice, I assure you. I'm sorry Grandmama gave you such a hard time. Actually she likes you very much."

"You jest."

"No, truly. She simply cannot bear not to know everything about a person. And she's never been foiled before."

"That I can well believe."

"I don't suppose I could persuade you to confide in her after all, or in me? Or Jesse? Someone, anyone. Sometimes a situation is not as serious as one thinks, and someone outside the problem may have a clearer view."

Anna shook her head sadly. "You mean to be kind, I know. The unhappy details of my past could serve no purpose and might even bring scandal to this house. Lies do a great deal of damage, even when they are exposed. Whatever happens to me, I will not let my problems bring harm to this family."

"I doubt Jesse would thank you for being so protective of him, ma'am. He's a pretty good man in a fight. No? Well, keep it in mind. One last question I would like you to consider very carefully. Is it at all possible that the attack on the coach was directed at you and not the heiress?"

"I have thought of it. But no, they must have been after the heiress. It makes no sense any other way."

"I'm not sure it makes sense at all. But come, let's join Jesse and Grandmama, and see if they can find anything significant in what I learned in town."

In the study, Lady Sarn was teaching Oliver card tricks. Doctor Abernathy had returned purportedly just to say hello, but in reality to check up on his patient, on Jesse's request. He was chatting calmly about recent village events to an inattentive host, whose eyes continually drifted to the open door.

Jesse would have been much surprised to know how many pairs of eyes were on him, silently calculating, as he watched Anna's return, looking for signs of distress.

"No browbeating at all, I promise you, Jess. Never even brought out the thumbscrews."

"I only wish I could have remembered something more helpful. I can't even give a good description of the thieves beyond their general size and the color of their eyes."

"Don't worry about it. We're lucky you are here to tell the story at all. There are still a few things we can look into."

"Have there been any reports of strange men in the area?" Jesse asked Sarn.

"Not yet, not other than the duke's wedding guests, but word of the attack is only just reaching the outlying areas now. I've sent a few of my men out to look for any likely hiding places where the thieves might have holed up—abandoned barns, that sort of thing."

"How did the girl's guardians take the news?" Jesse was glad to have avoided that ordeal.

"Surprisingly well. Too well, in fact. Would you believe it? They didn't even flinch when they viewed the body. I never thought an heiress could be an object of pity, but I sincerely pity that girl—and not only for the horrible way she died."

"They were able to identify the girl then?" Jesse hoped he didn't sound too surprised. There were some things best forgotten.

"Yes, from that small scar on her left arm. Miss Herries, you look surprised. What is it?"

"Nothing really. I was just thinking. If my memory of those voices is correct and the murder was not to be discovered, the body not found, then this clears the heiress's guardians. They could easily have denied recognizing the girl. After all, our own conclusion was only based on the letters and what I was told."

"Not only that, but it seems Sir John and his lady have nothing to gain from their charge's death. In fact, they stand to lose a good deal," the viscount added.

"Pity," Lady Sarn commented. "I could have pictured those two as a pair of villains. So, spill it, boy. Who gets all the lovely loot?"

"As far as I can tell, the only ones who are sure to make a profit out of the heiress's death are the members of the legal fraternity. I managed to get hold of the heiress's solicitor this morning, and he described the situation to me. It's a nightmare. First of all, the lady left no will."

"Surely that's odd—especially with so much money involved," Jesse said.

"Turnbull claims he urged the heiress to write a will time after time, but she refused."

"But wouldn't the guardians get the money, as next of kin?" Oliver's forehead wrinkled in confusion.

"They're not kin at all. Lady Ryland was the daughter of Ware's second wife by a previous marriage." Sarn waited a moment for this information to sink in. "The situation is then further complicated by the fact that there are actually three separate fortunes involved. I'll start with Ware's because that's the simplest. The old man evidently didn't trust his son's or daughter-in-law's management. Didn't believe in women handling money at all. So he left his fortune to his granddaughter in trust until she was either thirty years of age or married. The guardians got a very comfortable allowance, and were to get a bonus on the day the heiress wed. But if, as it happened, the lady died before marrying or turning thirty, the money reverts to the crown if there are no living Gallant relatives. The heiress's father was certainly believed to be the last of the line. Turnbull means to look into the possibility that the third marquess's second cousin, who left England in disgrace in 1694, may have surviving issue."

"Gadzooks!" said a wide-eyed Oliver.

"Gadzooks indeed. Then we come to the fortune amassed by his son Gareth, Lord Merton, in India. That was left to Lady Annabelle in trust until her twenty-fifth birthday. Since the heiress died without legitimate issue before that day, that money is now left to one of Lord Merton's cronies from his days in India, or the man's issue. The man was last heard of in the Kashmiri mountains. Did you say something, Oliver?"

"No. That is, no."

"Now we come to the heiress's third and last fortune—

the princely dowry given Elisabeth of Zschau and the royal family jewels. This fortune the heiress has had under her full control since her twenty-first birthday. But since she died intestate, without a will, they go to her closest living maternal relative—some elderly cousin who lives somewhere in the Carpathian mountains. The famous jewels which are part of this fortune disappeared at the time of Lord and Lady Merton's deaths and have not been seen since.''

"So the lawyers are now faced with trying to find a possible long-lost cousin of the Gallants, an adventurer lost among the wild tribes of the Kashmir, and an aged cousin of the heiress's mother isolated by Napoleon's hunger for conquest," Jesse summed up.

"Exactly. Now if somebody shows up claiming to be the long-lost cousin, etc., I would become awfully suspicious, but there's small likelihood that any of those people, assuming they're still alive, have the remotest idea that they stand in line to inherit."

"Wait up, Viv. The gel has an idea," Lady Sarn commanded.

"Excuse me, my lord, but this is what will happen to the money *now that the heiress is known to be dead*. But if the body had never been found, if she was thought to have simply disappeared?''

"Then the Rylands would keep their allowance for another five years. But if that were their purpose, why choose to identify the body?''

If Anna had an answer to that question, she kept it to herself.

Jesse gave Anna's hand a comforting clasp. "The murderer will make some kind of move, you'll see. If there is some scheme to get the money, he'll show his hand soon enough.''

"Well, we are not simply going to wait for something to happen," Sarn promised. "I'm not too proud to confess that this mare's nest is beyond my poor powers. I've never had to deal with any crime more serious than poaching before. Bow Street professionals are what's needed and, thanks to the generosity of lawyer Turnbull, that's what we're going to get. Not that that lets me off the hook. It will be at least another week before a runner can get here from London, so I'd better not leave any stone unturned in the meantime."

Feeling that it was about time someone lightened the atmosphere, Jesse asked, "And how does Miss Potterby feel about this prospective loss of attention from her newly acquired fiancé?"

"Miss Potterby is enthralled. I think I could have brought my courtship to a successful conclusion months ago if I'd had a case like this to dangle in front of her. To her nothing could be more romantic—a damsel in distress, and her hero chasing after the villains. If only I'd been the one to rescue Miss Herries as well. . . ."

"Anna rescued herself," Jesse remarked, a little severely. There was a flirtatious look in his newly affianced friend's eyes that he did not care for. "We were just lucky to be at the end of her trail."

"I was lucky you were at the end of my trail," Anna said in a low tone. Her hand, still resting in Jesse's, returned its warm clasp. Then, embarrassed, she pulled her hand free. In her heart she knew that this was not the end of her journey, nor could it be.

"Having agreed that fortune has been kind to you both, I must take my leave. The duke has agreed to lend me some of his men to help in the search. Poor man, he's quite shaken by the whole situation."

"His finances must be worse than we know," Lady Sarn commented darkly. "No wonder he's grieving—to come so close to all those millions and then to have a freak accident rob him of the prize when it was almost in his grasp! It's not as if he even knew the woman."

"They hadn't actually met, true. But Westerbrooke told me that they had corresponded for some time—ever since the alliance was first presented for consideration. He didn't claim their relationship was a great romance, but he did say he and the heiress had grown to be close friends and they had high hopes for their future together. Considering his past record with women, I thought he showed more real affection than I expected of him,'' Jesse said.

''Whatever his motives, the duke's help is very welcome. If there is any news, be assured you will be the first to know. I'll be by again to check on Grandmama's mischief-making in any case.'' Ignoring his elderly relative's rude comments, Sarn continued, ''I would like to bring my Chloe to call, if Miss Herries feels up to it. She's filled with admiration for your courage and is anxious to meet the heroine of the day.''

''Your fiancée is like to be very disappointed in finding an ordinary governess where she had hoped to find a heroine. But yes, I would be charmed to meet Miss Potterby.''

Lord Sarn bid a final adieu to the company and proceeded to the foyer with his host. Having cloaked himself carefully to protect his large frame against the chill breeze, Sarn prepared to step out the door when a breathless Anna ran up to halt him with a final question.

The continued presence of Jesse Norwood was something Anna had hoped to avoid, but obviously Jesse was not about to leave her alone to speak her mind privately. With an exasperated look in his direction, she addressed the viscount.

''My lord, I know there must be a great deal of gossip in the village about the heiress's death—and my survival. Should this talk reach the ears of the murderers, are they not likely to . . . to make another attempt to ensure that I remain silent? For myself I would not care, but I would never forgive myself if my presence brought danger to this house.''

Before Jesse could interject his forceful opinion on the subject, Lord Sarn intervened. ''Why, ma'am, if there is any danger, it is to the thieves, not from them. What you have already revealed of their crime is now generally known, and no act of theirs can retract it. They must also be aware how pitifully few details you can provide to lead to their identification. And indeed I doubt your highwaymen would worry overmuch at that anyway. Hired bravos such as these must be wanted on so many charges that one more can have little effect save enhancing their evil reputations among their brotherhood. No, you cannot harm them, so why should they waste more time over you? But they—they can identify the real villain, the person who hired them. And to my mind that situation makes for real danger. Popular superstition to the contrary, there is no honor among thieves.''

After the door had closed behind the viscount, Jesse's annoyance finally broke loose.

"You show a flattering degree of trust in our ability to protect you, ma'am. Perhaps you would feel safer somewhere else?"

There was pain in his eyes, as well as anger in his clenched fists. He thought she doubted his courage, his strength. To tell him he was too good, and, for all his years, too innocent of evil to cope with this threat would hardly soothe his hurt pride. Nor could she tell him that no woman will willingly risk the safety of her beloved, however much she may think of his talents for self-preservation. The thought of Jesse at the mercy of her enemies was too much to bear. It gave her the spurt of anger she needed to face him.

"Now you're hurt. I suppose you'd have liked nothing better than the opportunity to fight hordes of marauding invaders. Yes, I see you would. Well, I am sorry that my timid nature cannot face the idea of the Battle of Norwood Hall with equanimity."

Anna's acerbic tone quite robbed Jesse of any lingering anger. He was shrewd enough to hear some of the concern behind the words.

"My, my. How fierce you have become of late! And I had told Sarn what a peaceful person you were."

A smile tugged at her unwilling lips. "I'm afraid you are bearing the brunt of thirteen years of repressed sensibility." Thirteen years of loneliness, too. Would she feel differently if those years had been spent other than they were, if she had known happiness before, if she had known affection? Somehow, she thought not.

"I can bear it," Jesse answered.

Anna held her breath at the warmth she saw in his eyes. Trust he wanted—oh, she would trust him with her life. But with the truth? He thought he could handle anything; he was wrong. The truth was the one thing he could never accept, never believe. And when finally he did recognize it, would those eyes glow so warmly then? Anna feared not.

Her eyes, too, sent a silent message—to warn against trust, to warn him away. It was hard enough to face the hurt that must inevitably come no matter what form his farewell took, but at least he would never know how very much she cared. The familiar mask dropped back into place.

Jesse could feel her withdraw. He would have liked to shake her, to force Anna's careful wall of reserve aside and make her confide in him. But confidence cannot be forced. It must be given freely, without reservation. So the gentleman in Jesse acknowledged temporary defeat and led his guest back to the study, while a less respectable part of him vowed to continue the siege until the walls of her reserve were toppled at last.

chapter
VIII

That Miss Herries had other unexpressed reasons for fearing widespread knowledge of her present situation did not occur to her host. Less blinded by emotion, the dowager and her grandson did indeed consider the idea, but swiftly discarded it, as they were very nearly sure that the name Herries was not Anna's own. They did see, however, other dangers and possibilities in the gossip that was sure to result from Anna's prolonged stay.

To the curious neighbors of the surrounding area the strangest element of all in the mystery was the continued presence of a lady—any lady—at Norwood Hall. Since the day Baron Norwood "lost" his lady wife, no female outside the servant class (other than Lady Sarn) had been welcomed within the precincts of his country home. While the baron, however, was excused on the grounds that he would eternally mourn his lost love, Mr. Jesse Norwood was simply condemned as a renegade woman-hater. He never attended any of the local assemblies. When he could be induced to join a house party, he neither danced nor played cards, but discussed the foreign situation and the price of grain with his host. If he found the ladies lacking in sense, so too did they find him wanting, for he had no style, no small talk. In short, he lacked all the qualities and attentions that made a man agreeable—he could not flirt.

How then should such a man survive day-to-day contact with a member of the abhorred species—woman? To explain such strange hospitality on Mr. Norwood's part, it was therefore confidently reported in various quarters that the survivor of the attack was only a child, an aged grandmother, an incomparable beauty, and a boy in disguise. Jesse had either refused her entrance and been overruled by the doctor, or was being blackmailed by the woman. She was a witch and had put a spell on him. She was in league with the thieves. She was Jesse's mistress. She was the baron's cast-off mistress.

Anna was a grave disappointment to those who braved the inclement weather, the rough roads, and the rough side of Lady Sarn's tongue to come to see her. A poor sort of heroine this—meek as a nun, her eyes lowered, speaking only when spoken to, as unfashionable as the borrowed finery she wore. No one could doubt she had been a governess, only how she had been able to overcome her timidity to make her escape.

What made the exploratory visits worthwhile was the behavior of the lady's rescuers and chaperones. To see the stolid Mr. Norwood possessively protective, that high-stickler Lady Sarn pointedly affirming the girl's social equality, and even the boy Oliver ostentatiously careful of her well-being, was better than a play. One was, unfortunately, unable to glean much real information about the lady and her past, but obviously the dowager knew all the details—she always did.

That the county was expected to accept, nay welcome, this hitherto unknown governess was made quite clear. Perhaps the most telling indication of Miss Herries's place in the household was the attitude of the servants. From the first they had recognized Miss Anna as the real article, "quality." Now she was no longer simply a lady, but Mr. Jesse's lady, the natural mistress of his home.

Probably the only people doubtful of the eventual outcome of Miss Herries's advent on the scene were those most closely concerned. Nothing in his past life had prepared

Jesse Norwood for the onslaught of love. His charms had ever been rated lower than those of his titled brother by the husband-hunters and their mamas. While he knew Anna had no resemblance to that type of woman he despised, the damage to his self-esteem was already done.

The secrets, the seeming lack of trust, gnawed at him, as it did his friends. Jesse saw only a past full of pain, however. The dowager and the viscount feared nameless horrors and an inevitable separation.

Since the evening of the dowager's inquisition Anna had withdrawn further into herself. Her fears were private, unspoken. Lady Sarn hazarded a guess at the foremost of Anna's worries and invited her to stay as her ladyship's paid companion, for as long as Anna could put up with the dowager's whims or until she found a better situation. Her only answer was a surprising hug and kiss upon the cheek that left the crusty old lady so flustered that it was some time before she realized Anna had never said yes or no.

If Anna's reaction to the dowager's offer was ambiguous, Jesse's was not. His relief, however, was short-lived. He had long recognized Anna's prickly independent pride as a difficult hurdle facing anyone who wished to help her. That a few more uncomfortable virtues, other than her troublesome self-sufficiency, blocked the way to romance soon became apparent.

The announcement that the Bow Street Runners had at last arrived and would need to question Miss Herries yet again was greeted with a stoic calm that set off alarm bells in Jesse's mind. Finding Anna alone and pensive at the pianoforte, Jesse assayed the comfort he thought was needed.

"You know Viv and I, and Lady Sarn, will see to it that the Runners don't overstep the limits of this investigation. All you have to tell them is how you met the heiress and about the attack on the coach. Reliving that nightmare is quite bad enough, I'm sure. They'll not do any poking into your past beyond that point." It was his personal pledge he was giving, to protect her from unwonted curiosity.

"Will they not?" Anna sounded skeptical. Her right hand almost unconsciously picked out the melody of a Mozart concerto. When she realized what she was doing, she pulled her hand back into her lap and laughed uncomfortably. "I always play Mozart when I'm upset and need to think something through. Trying to capture some of that clarity and harmony for myself, I suppose." It helped to hide a multitude of emotions as well, such as her intense awareness of his presence, and allowed her to avoid his searching glance as he leaned over her music. One way or another, she swore inwardly, there must be an end to this.

Jesse waited patiently until the problem furrowing her brow should rise to the surface.

"These Runners—are they very good? I mean, can they actually find anything new, weeks after the event?"

"Vivian assures me that these are two of Bow Street's best investigators. As for the rest, who can say? But these men are professionals. Clues that might go unrecognized by us can mean a great deal to the trained mind. You must remember, too, that they will have sources of information about the criminal classes that we cannot even imagine."

"Yes, yes, that's so." Anna seemed comforted a little, but still her fingers reached out to play that same melody.

"It means that much to you—catching the blackguards who attacked the carriage?"

"I don't think I'll ever feel free until they're caught," she confessed, looking straight into Jesse's dark eyes.

This time Jesse caught the slim hand before it reached the keys of the pianoforte. "It's not your responsibility, Anna. You could not have stopped the attack from happening. You've done all you could to identify the killers. Nobody could expect you to do more."

"I can. I do. I keep thinking that I could do more—if I had the courage. But I'm so afraid, so afraid."

"You, afraid? I wish I could believe you had even enough native caution to prevent you from doing something dreadfully foolhardy."

A frightened determination to act was written on Anna's countenance, which in turn struck terror into Jesse's heart. There was very little Anna would not dare to do in the name of duty, he realized.

"Listen to me, Anna. I want you to promise me to give the Runners a chance at least. Whatever scheme you've got niggling at the back of your head can wait at least one week."

There was a long silence while he waited for her response.

"Very well, I promise. One week won't matter." Another lie. Every moment mattered when it might be all the love and happiness she would ever know. But she smiled bravely just the same.

With this Jesse, perforce, had to be content. But as he left the room, the strains of Mozart's music followed him.

That melody continued to haunt Jesse and trouble his thoughts through the dark hours of the night and into the sunlit hour that brought Lord Sarn and the Bow Street Runners to Norwood.

"She frightens me, Viv," Norwood confessed to his friend, while Lady Sarn chaperoned the interrogation.

"Be reasonable, Jess. What can she do?"

"What can she do? You ask that about a woman who fought a blizzard of monumental proportions, traveling miles with a bullet in her shoulder? What can't she do? For some reason Anna considers it her personal responsibility to capture the murderers. And nothing you or I can say can change her mind."

"Perhaps. But if you can think of any avenue of investigation we've ignored, I wish you will tell me."

Jesse kept his eyes on the blazing fire, struggling to keep emotion out of his voice. "Do you remember her asking if you thought there was any danger of further attack?"

"I do, and I still think Anna has nothing to fear from that quarter."

"What if she invited attack? Claimed to know more than she had told the authorities?"

"My dear fellow, the attackers, of all people, must know she can't identify them."

"Not them, no. But the real villain, the one who hired the cutthroats. Anna was alone with the heiress for hours. Suppose she claimed to know the motive for killing the girl?

What kind of reaction do you think a few indiscriminate hints at blackmail might provoke?''

"Bloody hell!"

"Exactly. My only hope is that either your two blood-hounds discover something in the next week or that I can somehow prevent Anna leaving Norwood. I know her well enough to realize that she won't risk endangering anyone else.''

"What are you going to do? Tie her down?''

"If necessary. I'm sorry to tell you that your grandmama is about to contract a dreadful case of the influenza and will need constant care.''

"If Grandmama is willing to take to her bed, the case must be serious,'' Lord Sarn conceded.

"Never doubt it. Find those killers, Viv. Find them before Anna offers them another victim.''

Very little finding proved to be necessary. The two thieves had surrendered to the tempting lure of a snowbank what they would not give up to the law. According to the shepherd who found them, they looked quite contented, as from a job well done.

"Still clutching some of their booty, so Zachary tells. We'll need Miss Anna to identify her things, but there's no doubt these are the men. Strangers to the area. The Runners think they're probably amateurs. They don't correspond to any description of known felons at least.'' Lord Sarn shrugged uncomfortably. He did not need the accusing glares of Anna and Jesse to tell him that this was not a satisfactory solution.

"Then there's an end to it.'' Anna's tone, carefully devoid of expression, sent shivers down the viscount's spine. No wonder Jesse was worried.

"No, certainly not. The Runners will simply have to find out who these men are . . . and see if they have any known connections with anyone close to the heiress, and so on.''

In actual fact, the Runners had shown no inclination to go any further in the matter at all. Hired bravos, if caught, could easily be turned over to the judicial process. "Nobs,'' as they termed the privileged class, were likely to find some way to escape punishment, making their apprehension so much wasted effort.

The derisive curling of Lady Sarn's lip told her grandson that he was not making the impression he desired.

"In any case," he hurried along, "the first step is to absolutely confirm that these are the two men who attacked the coach. I know you didn't see their faces, Miss Anna, but you can at least tell that they are of the same general build. And you'll be able to recognize your own personal articles that were recovered."

"Yes, of course," she answered absently. "When do you want me to go?"

"Now, if you will. The bodies have been taken to Doctor Abernathy's surgery in the village."

"I'll just get a wrap then."

The ride into the village was a grim one. Anna's calm assurance that she would not faint at the sight of two dead bodies sent the young maid, brought to satisfy convention, into a state bordering catatonic shock. Lord Sarn attempted to lighten the atmosphere with a highly embroidered account of how the shepherd Zachary had delivered his horrible tale, plodding into the viscount's mama's very elegant and exclusive tea party—but to no avail. Realizing no one was paying him any mind, Sarn's voice finally drifted off at what should have been the high point of his narrative (Mama being doused with water while performing her best faint). Jesse never took his eyes from Anna, who in turn remained glued to the window, impervious to drafts, drinking in the passing scene like a desert-dweller starved for water.

The look in Anna's eyes puzzled and frightened Jesse. The view from the coach was a pretty landscape, a moderately picturesque village scene. To Jesse it was beautiful because it was home. But what did Anna see in this single street of cottages and shops, in the small groups of neighbors going about their business, to bring such an expression of wonder to her ascetic face? Where had she been, what had been done to her, that the simple activities of everyday village life should seem strange and new to her?

The carriage stopped outside a tall town house dating

from the reign of Queen Anne, bearing witness to a long-deceased gentleman's mistaken belief that the proximity of so many noble families would result in fashionable expansion for the little village. That long-ago gentleman had soon realized his mistake and the monument to his folly had passed from hand to hand, gradually coming down in he world until it now served as both residence and place of business for Doctor Abernathy.

Within the building there was far more evidence of surgery than home. An odor of camphor permeated every room. The large, comfortable woman who acted as housekeeper was just as often called upon to act as nurse-assistant. She led the party into a large room at the back of the ground floor in a cheerful fashion that indicated the presence of corpses was, to her, a matter of no concern.

Although she chatted with the viscount and Jesse Norwood, all the while giving Anna a discreet yet thorough inspection, she failed to mention that others had come upon the same fearful errand and were presently with the doctor. Prepared for grim duty and lost in private reflections, Anna was startled by the sudden appearance of two examples of the most extreme and foolish in London fashion. Her first reaction to their cool appraisal through matching lorgnettes was to shrink back out of sight, but her equanimity was restored by a whispered reminder of the dowager's acerbic character sketches.

Sir John Ryland and his Lady undoubtedly were perceived as figures of fun in country society where the ever present demands of the land continually reminded one of reality and responsibility. In town, however, they were in their element. Social cunning and a taste for intrigue took the place of intelligence and generosity, but in the Rylands' chosen sphere those mean talents served them well, as many an overconfident aspirant to the *ton* sadly discovered.

Anna's tense shoulders relaxed as the Rylands, having concluded she was a person of no consequence, focused instead on Lord Sarn as the only member of the party whose wealth and rank made him worthy of their attention. That the viscount and his companions found the baronet and his lady particularly repulsive was far beyond that couple's narrow perceptions.

Confident of a warm welcome (for surely my lord must long for livelier company in this tedious backwater?), Sir John advanced mincingly.

"My gracious lord, you find us engaged in a most grim and distasteful duty—the same, no doubt which has brought you to this awful place that reeks of mortality." Sir John managed to give his speech the flavor of rich pulpit oratory, but he could not match the somber tone of his voice with a corresponding gravity of demeanor. His eyes showed a distressing tendency to twinkle cheerfully, and his thin lips curved up more often than not.

"My husband is so clever, my lord, you can't imagine," Lady Ryland simpered. "When we heard the murderers had been found—dead—I thought everything would be over, but Sir John said to me, 'Mug'—that's what he calls me—'Mug, we must see if we can recognize these felons. Perhaps we can discover who was behind the attack on our (theatrical sob) beloved niece.' "

"And could you?"

"Alas, no," Sir John answered quickly. "And we had so hoped for some clue. I am right in thinking, am I not, that a known connection with these felons would heavily implicate someone . . . someone with a motive . . . in the murder?"

"I would say so, yes. Providing, of course, that it can be proved that these men are the murderers. We hope that Miss Herries will be able to give us exactly that assurance."

"Ah, the young lady who was in the coach with our dear Belle and who escaped so spectacularly." The bubbling cheerfulness finally faded from Sir John's voice, to be replaced with a tense wariness.

"The last person to see our little girl—for she was like our very own, you know—alive. And to hear her last words. Tell us, did she speak of her aunt and uncle? Did she leave one last message for her loved ones?" Lady Ryland asked nervously.

Both Sir John and Lady Ryland eyed Anna closely as she answered.

"I wish I could offer you some comfort, but we spoke very little, except to remark on the weather. And she talked about being married. That's all."

The Rylands relaxed, only to be startled anew by a question from the hitherto glowering and silent Jesse.

"I take it you have already recognized your niece's belongings?"

"Yes, I should like a written statement to that effect, if you please, Lady Ryland. The garments, etc., will be returned to you as soon as possible," Sarn, in his official capacity as magistrate, told them.

Lady Ryland looked at the small bundle of feminine attire—drab and much-mended merinos fit only for a governess, a few pretty gowns that were the height of fashion three or more years ago and that showed signs of alterations—and burst into tears.

"There, there, my dear, don't distress yourself. This has been a very trying period for my lady, Sarn. She ought to rest. Come, Mug dear, let us go back to the inn. . . ."

"The inn?" Sarn asked, surprised. Why weren't they at Westerbrooke?

"Yes. Such is Lady Ryland's sensibility that the continual reminder of what might have been has preyed distressingly on her nerves. Yet until your investigation was completed it seemed heartless to return to town. An old friend has just arrived, so we will stay another few days if you have any further questions for us. If not, however, we will be off soon. And try to find some consolation among our friends."

After Sir John removed his still weeping wife, Doctor Abernathy crossed to the casement and opened the windows, despite the chill bite to the air. "Keeping my mouth shut and not giving them a piece of my mind is just possibly the most difficult thing I've ever had to do."

Jesse growled expressively.

"My thoughts precisely," said Lord Sarn. "Did you see their expressions when I asked about the heiress's clothes? They hadn't the least idea what might be hers. I wonder how long it's been since they actually saw her? Well, Miss

Anna, can you identify your personal belongings among these?''

''Yes.'' Anna separated a very few drab articles from the pile. ''These are mine.''

Jesse fingered one of the remaining gowns.

''You look as if you'd never seen a lady's gown before, Jess,'' Sarn told him. ''Now, I know you're not such a hermit as all that.''

''Viv, look at this. I may know nothing of fashion, but even I can see that these gowns are well-worn, to say the least. Not what you'd expect the well-dressed heiress to have.''

''You're right. The style is a few years old as well. Chloe said something about seamstresses at the duke's mansion being expected to produce a complete trousseau in a week. One gathers the heiress lived . . . in seclusion. Her school is in an isolated part of the country. Still, it is strange.''

''I wonder what happened to the other horses,'' Anna said unexpectedly.

''Horses?'' the men asked in unison.

''Even if, as I suppose, the animals got away from the thieves, they couldn't get any farther than the men in that weather. Between the attackers' mounts and the carriage team, that's six horses to be accounted for—dead or alive. Only two were found.''

The gentlemen looked at Anna blankly.

''Well, come, Miss Anna,'' said the doctor kindly, ''and see if these men could have been your attackers, not that there's much doubt of that. They've been laid out for burial so they won't be an affright to your sensibilities. Died very peaceful anyway, just laid down in the snow and went to sleep forever.'' He pulled the sheets covering the bodies back.

''They do look . . . somehow familiar,'' Anna confessed. Her expression was perplexed. ''And yes, they are the same general build as the murderers. The spokesman was tall, slender, almost elegant. And the other was smaller, thin and wiry.'' She took a scarf and held it over the lower half of one face but was not satisfied by the results. "Their eyes are closed, Doctor. What color are they?"

"Hmmm? Oh, blue, both of them. Classical type of Saxon."

"No."

"But I assure you, they are."

"I mean, no, these are not the men who held up our coach. One of the thieves had gold eyes—too unusual to forget or to be mistaken. And the other's were dark, almost opaque. No, I'm sorry, but these are not the villains."

chapter
IX

"You'd better be right about tonight, Jesse, or I promise you I will personally tear you limb from limb. And Chloe will scratch your eyes out. On a lovely moonlit evening like this, I should be with my sweetheart, whispering words of romance into her shell-shaped ear—not keeping cold vigil with you in a smelly stable in the unlikely event that a woman of sense, of modesty and decorum, is suddenly going to behave like a lunatic! It's you who are insane. And I am, too, for agreeing to stay with you and freeze my. . . ."

Jesse and Lord Sarn were huddled over a small brazier in the stables at Norwood. The viscount insisted on the fire, asserting that even if Anna noticed the light she would only assume one of the grooms was watching over an ailing mare. Jesse had already conceded that Anna had not ridden since she was a child and therefore would most likely bypass the stables and cover the distance to the village by foot. While the two gentlemen could cover any exit from the rear of the Hall from their vantage point, Oliver and one of the footmen kept watch over the front entrance.

"She'll not come, I tell you," Sarn still insisted an hour later. "Why should she? The case is closed. The murderers are dead and there's nothing more to be learned."

"The murderers are not dead—at least, if they are we haven't discovered their bodies. If Anna says those two are not the men, they are not the men."

"Because of the color of their eyes? Piffle! Anna was in the middle of a blizzard and fighting for her life. How could she tell what color their eyes were? Or are you going to tell me we had two sets of thieves roaming around our little village that night and one stole the loot from the other?"

Sarn's sarcastic laugh was interrupted.

"By Jove, that's it!"

"Oh no, oh no. Jesse, how much of that flask have you drunk?"

"Don't you see? When Anna told of the attack she was confused about the voices. The voices of the men who 'buried' them and those of the murderers didn't match."

"You see now why I think she's mistaken. The poor girl was obviously in shock at the time."

"She was clear-sighted enough to rescue herself—and, I might add, is only confused about what happened *after* she was shot, not before."

"Dammit, Jess, I don't want another murderer. I could hardly handle one."

"It's hardly a matter of what you or I want. It's the only thing that makes sense. Tawny eyes and dark eyes attack the coach and kill the heiress. Probably they're interrupted while they are still searching for the letters, before they have done anything with the bodies. So they hare off, taking the horses. Then our two unfortunate blue-eyed Saxons come along on the same errand and find their work's already been done for them. All they've to do is dispose of the bodies—as Anna overhears. But the storm has become much worse and they don't make it . . . wherever they meant to go."

"There's not much out Zachary's way."

"Where they were found means less than nothing. I wouldn't have trusted myself to find these stables without getting lost that night."

"I suppose." The viscount shivered glumly.

"You see, it does make sense. It also brings up some interesting questions."

"Such as? No, I don't think I want to know."

"Too bad. First, if the original attackers got away alive, they're still in the area. The roads have been watched, and they couldn't go far at all cross-country," Jesse reasoned quietly.

"Zachary's was the last place to be searched. Where do you think they're hiding then?"

"In the open. With a perfectly good reason to have an extra team on hand."

"At the inn?"

"Or the duke's." Jesse grinned at his friend's shocked expression. "Possibly at Sarn. . . ."

"Possibly . . . !"

"Another matter to consider is whether both sets of murderers wanted the evil deed covered up. The two gentlemen lying in state in Robert's surgery evidently were under orders to bury the evidence. Who knows, had the horses not been stolen already they might simply have driven the carriage away. We've been assuming that the first pair of killers were searching for proof of the heiress's identity, but that theory was based on a single pair of villains."

"Oh. I see. I think. But what else could they have been looking for? They must have been very well-informed beforehand."

"Well done, Viv. You're quite right. They weren't just searching randomly for a few extra golden boys. There was something specific they were ordered to find."

"Yet all the heiress hid were those letters."

Jesse's gasped "I told you so" covered the last part of the viscount's sentence.

Following the line of Jesse's pointed finger, Sarn could see a dark figure against the snow, brought into focus by the bobbing lantern carried in her hand.

"Lud, you were right! Females! There's no understanding them. Not that I'm complaining, mind."

"Hush. Sounds carry far on these cold, clear nights."

The viscount experienced some difficulty in heeding

this command, especially when he realized that Jesse intended that they follow on foot rather than mounted. Despite his sometimes frivolous and lazy attitudes, however, Sarn well realized the gravity of the situation. Even were murder not involved, anything that mattered so very much to Jesse Norwood must be treated with the utmost respect.

The light Anna carried made pursuit simple. The security of Jesse's steps indicated that he had a good idea where she was heading, too. Sarn said as much when the late-night sounds of the village offered some cover for his voice.

"I told you before what I thought she would do if your investigation failed. The choice of victim seems pretty obvious," Jesse answered.

The choice was not at all obvious to the viscount, but he made no comment. They watched Anna hide her lantern so it could be easily retrieved.

A coach full of revelers passed them on its way back to the duke's mansion. Sounds of merriment issued from the inn, where not long ago Jesse had first told his friend and the dowager about the outrage in the storm.

The reaction to weeks of forced inactivity had not yet passed. Guests of the duke, deprived of wedding festivities, sought elsewhere for diversion. Business was very brisk indeed, so brisk that a "serving maid" might go about her business quite unnoticed.

Jesse walked confidently up the stairs to the private rooms.

"How do you expect to be able to eavesdrop? I can just see you, ear to the keyhole, having the door open in your face."

"No need to do that. I've no doubt at all Anna will confide the whole to us afterward. It's her physical safety I'm worried about," said Jesse.

"Why did we have to stalk her like a cuckolded husband in a farce then?" Sarn muttered.

"If we'd faced her, Anna would have let us talk her out of it. And then she'd have tried again when she was sure we weren't watching. Or worse, she'd leave Norwood entirely."

The inn was a very old building, its corridors suddenly leading up or down a few steps, taking unexpected turns. Jesse was just about to comment on the best and safest vantage point to observe the door to the private parlor that had been Anna's goal when the need for secrecy was abruptly destroyed. The door flew open and there stood Anna, pale and trembling. The realization of Jesse's perfidy in following her might sink in later, but now there was only a deep sense of relief. She stumbled into his open arms and hid her face in his shoulder. For some moments she could not utter a word. All too soon, to Jesse's mind, Anna was able to regain control of her shuddering frame. Stepping out of his comforting embrace, she raised large, frightened eyes to his and said the horrible word. "Murder. They've been poisoned."

"Did you move or touch anything?" Jesse demanded, deliberately keeping his voice brusque.

"No, nothing. I . . . couldn't."

"Fine. What I want you to do, Anna, is go and get Robert Abernathy—you remember where the surgery is? He's used to being roused at all hours, so that won't matter. Send him to us here. You wait for us at the surgery."

Anna was too shaken to take umbrage at Jesse's dictatorial manner. Having someone take control at this point was a relief.

After she had pulled her hood to cover her face and departed inconspicuously down the stairs, Sarn ventured to hiss, "Should we let her go alone?"

"She walked here from Norwood alone. A few minutes alone in the cold air will give her time to pull herself together. Did you mean anything else? You don't—you can't suspect Anna?"

"You're the one who's been insisting that the murderers are still on the loose. How do you know Anna hasn't decided to try her story on someone else, without benefit of escort?"

Luckily for Jesse's peace of mind, the doctor soon appeared and assured the gentlemen that Anna had been left in the capable hands of his housekeeper. Anna would not escape that lady's vigilance and curiosity.

Anna had not the strength of will to run. She shivered in the warm study and answered haphazardly the curious housekeeper's questions. Obediently she finished her cup of tea and then another. And all the while her mind was fixed on a single moment at the inn—the moment when Jesse's arms had reached for her and held her safe. In the terror of discovering the Rylands dead, her only thought had been an intense longing for Jesse. Had she cried his name aloud? Had she revealed what most of all must be hidden?

But he'd been there, her heart reminded her again and again. She needed him and he was there.

After what seemed an interminable wait and innumerable cups of tea later, Anna was rejoined by the gentlemen.

The doctor was furious. "How dare the villain! How dare he involve *my* surgery! My medicines! But he'll pay for it. That's where he made his mistake—he stole the wrong bottle!"

"I don't understand. What happened?" Anna asked. She was still pale but no longer trembling.

"It was supposed to look like a suicide, we think. Due to either remorse for killing the heiress, or fear that they were about to be found out," Jesse explained, sitting next to Anna and taking her hand as if to assure himself of her safety. "But our murderer was a little too clever. In order to make it seem obvious that the Rylands had taken the poison deliberately, and not just succumbed to a bad meat pie. . . ."

"At the Blue Boar? That's an insult to Mrs. Huckaby's fine cooking," said Lord Sarn.

". . . a bottle, well-marked with skull and crossbones was placed next to the wine bottle. The Rylands would have had the opportunity to pinch the stuff when they were here earlier in the afternoon," Jesse continued over the interruption.

"They would not," the doctor disagreed. "Either Mary or I kept an eye on them every minute. Didn't like the looks of them. Stupid thing to do anyway. Why risk stealing when you can find anything you need in your own garden? Even some of the rat poison Huckaby uses in the stables would be easier to get.''

''It may not have been the easy thing, but why wrong?'' Anna asked the doctor to clarify his ravings.

''For one thing, there was less than half a bottle of this before it was stolen. I had reason to check it just yesterday, so I know. All that's been poured out of here is a little to show there's poison—this poison—in each wineglass. The other thing is that all poisons don't act alike. Some distillations are poisonous only when overdosed; in small amounts the effect may be quite beneficial.''

''What Robert is trying to say, in his long-winded fashion, is that this stuff wouldn't kill them,'' Sarn translated.

''Would not kill them so quickly,'' the doctor testily corrected him. ''An entire bottle of this might do for them. But they'd be sick as dogs for a good few hours first.''

''With time aplenty to call the doctor and put an end to any foolish ideas about suicide,'' added Jesse.

''And it had to be suicide, not an accident, in order to finish the investigation into the heiress's murder,'' Anna said.

''Quite. You called it murder right away, I understand, Miss Anna. What tipped you off?'' Doctor Abernathy asked.

All three gentlemen turned to observe her curiously.

''I hardly know. Except I knew in my heart they would never think of killing themselves. Well, you saw what they were like. If anything, they were elated this afternoon, like children with a secret. 'I know something you don't know.' ''

''And you thought you could threaten them into telling you—whatever it was.'' Jesse sounded thoroughly disgusted.

''Oh yes. They weren't very bright. Perhaps they wouldn't be dead now if they'd been a little more farsighted.''

''And a little less greedy,'' Jesse added.

''Blackmail, do you mean?'' The idea had not occurred to the viscount before, and he rather wished it would go away now. ''Haven't we enough crime already with theft and multiple murders?''

''Come on, Viv. Face facts. Those two are dead because they knew something. Given the choice between helping the authorities avenge the heiress's death or lining their own pockets, which do you think they'd pick?''

"Damn. They didn't waste any time, did they—the blackmailers or the murderer?''

"Do you know how they spent the day, after they left us in the surgery?'' Anna asked quietly.

"A little shopping. Anticipating the extra income, I suppose. Then back to the inn. And they stayed in the private parlor all evening, as far as Huckaby knows,'' Sarn answered.

"But he couldn't really know, not with the crowd in there tonight. And anybody could have popped up from the taproom without being noticed as well.'' Anna knew from her own experience.

"Surely we can eliminate the locals,'' the doctor protested. "It would have to be someone they knew.''

"The whole crowd from the duke's wedding party was there, Robert, the duke included. Even that lawyer fellow was still there. But damned if I can see why any one of them would want to kill the heiress. They'd never even met her. And had no chance at the money.'' Jesse was beginning to sound tired.

"Someone who wanted the duke free to marry another?'' Anna was shy about suggesting so romantic a possibility.

"Humph. From what Chloe and her mama tell me, Westerbrooke's position in the Marriage Mart is hard to judge. The high-sticklers don't care for his morals, his companions, or his propensity for games of chance. Nor is there a lot of respect for these new creations. On the other hand, the only difference between the duke's behavior and that of any other Corinthian is that he's less discreet. The girls find those golden curls and golden eyes very romantic. But, more to the point, the females with whom Westerbrooke has been known to associate have no expectation other than financial ones.'' When Sarn realized what he had said and to whom, he had the grace to blush. He tried to cover up his embarrassment by quickly adding, "Huckaby has given me a list of all the guests, overnight and taproom business, that he can recall. We questioned just about everyone that was sober enough to pay attention, with the exception of a schoolmistress and her charge who only arrived today. But since we have proved that someone could sneak in and out without being seen,'' this with a darkling look at Anna, "you can imagine how much value this testimony has.''

Jesse, having observed Anna grow paler and more chillingly quiet by the moment, chose to hasten their departure from the doctor's home. There was no further action that could be taken until the morrow. To continue would be merely to indulge in idle and fearful speculation.

A gig from the inn had been bespoken to carry the trio home. The doctor added a warm blanket to cover their limbs. When Jesse saw Anna shivering in the night air, however, he wrapped it solicitously about her, ignoring both his own discomfort and that of the viscount.

The return drive was accomplished in silence, broken only at the gates of Norwood Hall by the viscount's refusal to spend the night.

"No, I must go on. If I don't, Lord knows when I'll see Chloe again.''

"My Lord, Jesse.'' Anna, having been helped to dismount, held a hand out to each of the gentlemen and addressed them earnestly. "Thank you, both. I ought to be very angry with you for following me . . .''

Both made foolish attempts to deny that they had done any such thing and were ignored.

"I thought I could handle the situation. But this . . . I never was so glad to see anyone as I was to see you.''

The gentlemen were quite unable to know how to handle her gratitude. They would have felt more comfortable with the scold she had considered and they had expected. Jesse covered his embarrassment by immediately tending to the horses. Sarn countered with a change of subject.

"Miss Anna, just tell me, please. How the . . . blazes you meant to threaten those poor scoundrels into telling you anything?''

"Oh. I should think it almost certain that the Rylands have been stealing funds from the heiress's estate, don't you? No wonder they turned to blackmail so easily. I expect that will be given as a reason for their supposed guilt in the murder and subsequent suicide—the embezzling, I mean.''

"Well, I may not be much of an officer of the law, but I won't let these murders get passed off that way. Tomorrow I question the sobered-up patrons. And who knows? Maybe that schoolteacher—what's her name, Jess?''

"Mrs. Julia Thynne.''

"This Mrs. Thynne may have seen. . . . Anna! Help me, Jess. She's fainted!''

chapter X

Doctor Abernathy had been dragged away from his examination of the two latest corpses to see once again to Anna, who was greatly embarrassed by her sudden weakness the night before. Although the doctor had been gentleness personified when dealing with the shaken woman, he was rather more brusque with the equally upset Jesse. To the disturbed lover's request for an account of her condition, the doctor answered, "Well, if you can only keep her from sneaking out in the middle of the night to find more dead bodies, she will do very well." This attitude Jesse found offensive, not to say unjust. Some time was spent in an acrimonious exchange, until Anna, who refused to stay abed, interrupted with a demand for more information.

There was little to be told. Abernathy confirmed that he believed the Rylands had been dead for some hours when they were at last discovered. Since incapacitation, if not death, must have been virtually immediate, the poison was probably ingested with the evening meal. The obnoxious Londoners had already so offended the innkeeper that even had they rung for help or for further service, they ran the risk of being ignored. The operative question now was: did the murderer have to be present at the time the poison was taken, or could the murderer have merely sent a poisoned substance to the Rylands, something like wine or sweets, any time during the day?

No trace of the poison that had actually been used to kill the Rylands remained in the rooms. Lady Ryland had bought sweets on her earlier promenade among the shops, but there was no sign of even a wrapper now. The dinner dishes had been left on a tray outside the room and subsequently cleaned to a shine by the scullery maid. Huckaby, afraid for the reputation of his establishment, commented that the considerate act of setting the dinner tray outside should have warned him something was wrong.

Anna commented calmly on the housewifely aspect in the careful cleaning up of clues. The doctor had noticed this as well but did not care to mention it, especially in Jesse's presence. That circumstance might easily direct suspicion in the matter toward Miss Herries, especially if her moonlight visit should become generally known. The murderer might not necessarily have to administer the poison personally, but he or she did have to return to clear away the real evidence and replace it with the manufactured clues. Jesse would say Anna did not have enough time, but Jesse was in love with her. As a trusted friend, Anna would not have been so closely observed and might have purloined the marked bottle from the surgery. She was more closely connected to the heiress's murder than anyone else. If Anna could not be suspected of complicity in that first murder, she could be thought to have a strong motive now in her desire to avenge it. Jesse had often commented that Anna found the idea of the mystery left unresolved, the crime unpunished, an unbearable one. Oh yes, one could build quite a reasonable case against Miss Herries. He didn't believe a word of it. No one who knew her could. But someone who neither knew her nor cared about her could use theories, some real information, and the lack of information about Anna's past, against her.

Anna left soon, unaware of the doctor's fears, to tend to Lady Sarn, who was doing her part in preventing Anna from finding time to brood. The dowager's quick mind had already considered all the possibilities the doctor imagined and was equally frightened, for she knew another scapegoat would become necessary. Most of all, however, she feared Anna's reaction to any suspicion and wondered what Anna would do to preserve the secret of her past.

Jesse was probably alone in his complete ignorance of the ambiguity of Anna's position. Even Oliver put aside his disappointment at missing the exciting turn of events to worry for his new friend.

Lord Sarn, driving up the long approach to the Hall, had the most frightening thought of all. Perhaps the information the Rylands had tried to turn to advantage was not their recognition of the deceased highwaymen, but their recognition of Anna and knowledge of her true identity. A secret Anna deemed certain to doom her relationship with Jesse might well appear—to others—a strong enough motive for murder. That Sarn himself refused to consider Anna as a possible suspect mattered little. Like the others he realized that a scapegoat was still needed and would no doubt be provided.

The viscount was careful to hide these feelings, however, not only from his enamored friend but also from his enamored fiancée, who had accompanied him with the expressed desire of visiting Lady Sarn and an unexpressed curiosity to see the cause of so much furor.

Chloe Potterby was a diminutive brunette with big brown eyes and uncontrollably curling hair. Although she was only a few years older than Oliver, she was older by far both in knowledge of the world and wisdom of the heart. As the youngest of a large family she had learned to stand up for herself very early. She loved Sarn to distraction and was clever enough never to let him see how completely she ruled him.

Chloe's charm was irresistible. Even the misogynist Jesse, worn by anxiety, was forced to answer her warm smile. The doctor, who had not yet left, went so far as to give the viscount a wink of approval.

"Lady Sarn and Anna are upstairs," Jesse explained as the guests divested themselves of wraps and followed him into the drawing room. "Since Anna refused to rest, Lady Sarn has kept her busy sorting her silks."

"Sorting silks is one of Grandmama's favorite activities when she is worried or puzzled. She never embroiders. Hasn't the patience for it. So I can only assume that she lets the cats get at the silks as soon as she has them in order again."

"Very soothing. She told me it helps her think," Chloe said, giving Oliver a blinding smile as he offered her a chair. "Well, I see my nursing talents will not be needed. When Vivian told me that Miss Anna had fallen ill last night, I thought I might help by sitting up with her during the afternoon."

"Fallen ill, indeed!" Sarn spoke over his friends' polite expression of thanks. "You needn't be so mealymouthed. She fainted from the shock, and so would you. Chloe knows the whole," he explained. "In fact, she has some information of her own to contribute."

"It's the strangest thing. But it seems that I went to the same academy as the heiress!"

"And the headmistress was none other than the Mrs. Julia Thynne who is presently staying at the Blue Boar!" Sarn cut in.

"What an amazing coincidence! But I thought Viv told me you went to school in Bath. The heiress was at some place near one of the new mill towns, I thought," Jesse said.

"That's true. Mrs. Thynne's academy is quite close to my Aunt Augusta's house, which is how I came to go there. Mother had gone to India to be with my eldest sister for her lying-in, and I was sent to stay with Aunt Augusta. Poor dear, she didn't know what to do with me, so she enrolled me as a day pupil at this school."

"You knew the heiress then?" Oliver asked.

"That's the odd thing. Admittedly, I wasn't there very long, but I did meet all the girls, and I'd swear there was no one named Gallant there. And you'd expect her to be pointed out, wouldn't you?"

"Perhaps she was there under another name," the boy suggested. "As a safeguard."

"Perhaps." Miss Potterby sounded doubtful. "But it's awfully hard to keep a secret like that among a large group of young girls."

"That's the place you said you hated so much, isn't it?" Sarn asked.

"Mother thinks I disliked it because it was the first time I was away from home, but I honestly don't think that was why. It really was the oddest place, not at all . . . comfortable. It was impossible to get close to anyone or make friends. The headmistress watched over us like a hawk—not just to see that we behaved or did our lessons, but who we talked to and for how long. There was a music mistress there who played the pianoforte like an angel. I used to sneak in and listen while she practiced. Those were the only happy moments I ever spent there. And that is what got me in trouble. The poor music teacher . . . I wish I could remember her name . . . she didn't even know I was there, but she was treated horribly when I was discovered listening to her. As if it were her fault. And Mrs. Thynne scolded me terribly as well. She tried to reprimand Aunt Gussy, too, for not bringing me up properly, but there she went too far. Aunt Gussy took me out of the school immediately and took me on a tour of the Lake District instead."

"You see what this means, don't you?" Sarn asked.

"Your disinterested witness may not be so disinterested after all," said Jesse.

"Probably she has no more to do with the affair than half of the duke's guests who were getting so determinedly drunk last night. But I can't be sure. Lud, I keep praying for one, just one, person that can be completely excluded from the case!"

"And he can't even exclude me," Chloe teased with a twinkle in her eye, but with genuine sympathy.

"Anna and Lady Sarn will have to hear this," said Oliver with enthusiasm.

"Oh Lord, yes. Grandmama will never forgive us for not

telling her first. She can't bear not to know everything. Find them, will you, Noll?''

Oliver had half risen from his seat, and Chloe was in the midst of expressing her eagerness to meet the heroine of so many adventures, when the ladies appeared, evidently having been advised by the servants of the presence of guests. After dutifully saluting her future grandmama, Chloe turned to be presented to Anna when she stopped herself and everyone else cold in their tracks.

''Miss Herries. Why, of course, no wonder the name seemed so familiar. I was just telling Mr. Norwood about hiding in the corner to listen to you play. And I thought I had wangled all the facts out of Viv. He never mentioned you had been at school with the heiress. Isn't this the most amazing coincidence?'' She turned her bright, cheerful face to an audience that seemed to have turned to stone.

Jesse was the first to recover his voice, although it was barely recognizable. ''You lied. You said you never knew her. You lied to us.''

The anguish in his eyes was mirrored in Anna's. That which she had feared most had come to pass. The man who had held her lovingly in his arms but hours ago now looked upon her with cold disdain. She spoke directly to him as if there were no one else in the room. ''You knew I was hiding my past. That was my only real deception, I swear it.'' The disbelief, the disgust and sense of betrayal she read in his glance goaded her to cry out. ''There are six people dead because of me, because of my wretched inheritance! Would you have had me endanger more innocent people?''

The silence thickened as the implications of her cry sank in.

''I don't believe it,'' Jesse said. But his denial lacked force.

''I do.'' Lady Sarn wore a look of smug satisfaction. Finally her mystery was resolved. ''You've a look of your mother about the eyes. I knew your face was familiar.''

''And that sad story about the wicked employer? I suppose that was true as well—an heiress working as a governess? While you were Mrs. Thynne's prize pupil, no doubt.''

"Don't look away from me, Jesse. You blame me for not telling the truth, yet you will not accept it. After all that you have seen, how can you still hold on to that frivolous image of the society coquette? Do the garments from the coach show how many thousands of guineas I spend on my wardrobe? Does society ring with stories of my conquests? Did Sir John and Lady Ryland impress you with their careful attention to their duty as guardians?"

"They didn't recognize you."

"How should they? They haven't seen me since I was twelve."

"It happens," Lady Sarn said in a quiet tone. "More often than we know. And the greater the fortune involved, the more greed it engenders. The girls suffer most. The boys usually only have to wait for their majority, and hope the money won't be all gone. The girls either wait for a wedding that never comes or find themselves delivered into the hands of a bridegroom as unscrupulous as the guardians. And they still cannot touch their own inheritance."

"Mrs. Thynne's . . . ?" Chloe's mere mention of the name caused Anna to shiver.

"Mrs. Thynne's 'Academy' is a well-disguised prison for unwanted children. She has earned quite a reputation, well-deserved I must say, for keeping children out of the way and out of contact with others. There was one escape when I was first there—an older girl. She was caught, of course. And charged with theft. Mrs. Thynne had hoped to take the entire school to the hanging, but the girl's sentence was commuted to transportation to the colonies." Bitterly she added, "Didn't you think it at all odd that a woman of twenty-five years should still live at school?"

In self-defense Sarn remarked, "There could have been other reasons for keeping the heiress out of society." He paused. "The doctor could not help but know that the other woman had borne a child."

Anna recognized the justice of his reasoning.

"But I never knew. There were some students who were treated well, even toadied," Chloe protested.

"Oh yes. Mrs. Thynne wanted the prestige of a truly fine

school as well. And the real students served to cover her other activities. She also wanted to introduce her daughter, Caroline, into a better class of society. That was my salvation.''

''Salvation?'' Sarn asked.

''When I was brought there, Mrs. Thynne sent me to work in the scullery. I persuaded her that if she would allow me to pursue my studies, she would profit more by the use of an unpaid teacher. From having lived abroad I spoke fluent French and Italian. I had been well instructed in music, drawing, and the etiquette of court life. All the 'extras,' in fact, which increase the cost of tuition.''

''And she made you hide your identity, and use another name?'' Oliver asked.

''No, that was my guardians' idea. The fee would have been greater had Mrs. Thynne known who I really was. I have wondered if she found out somehow. In the last four years, her treatment grew more and more cruel, as if she hated me. That's why I decided to seem to acquiesce to the wedding arrangements.''

''You'd have turned him down otherwise?'' Jesse asked, his voice floating out from the shadowy corner where he stood. There was no disbelief or sarcasm in his voice now, but Anna had grown too numb to notice the change.

''Oh, I never meant to go through with it. Any marriage arranged by my guardians must be suspect. But it did offer a chance to escape, once released from Mrs. Thynne's care. And I must admit to being curious. I still cannot imagine what forced my guardians into arranging this marriage. The duke is not one of their cronies.''

Anna was seated now, tired and more than a little withdrawn, a picture of the demure governess. After her outburst she had ceased to look for Jesse and merely stared at her hands, clasped tightly in her lap. ''Is there anything else you need to know?''

''The facts of the attack were just as you told us?'' Sarn asked gently.

''Yes. Except that it was my chaperone who ran off after going through my luggage. She probably wanted to escape Mrs. Thynne, too.''

"And the other woman?"

"Her name was Annabelle also. We remarked on the coincidence. But she was Belle, and I was always just plain Anna. I suppose that's what gave me the idea of saying she was the heiress. Gantt was her name. Mrs. Edward Gantt. We talked very little. The one time she became animated was when she mentioned her son. For the rest I can only give my impressions—that her husband was . . . unsatisfactory, had possibly abandoned her. And she was frightened about her son's future. But that's only a guess. The ring was hers. 'They shan't have it,' she said." Anna took it off her finger where she had worn it since the day she had first told the story of the attack.

Sarn picked the ring up and read the inscription within. " 'May 3, 1801 Love Edward.' I suppose it's still unlikely that the attack had anything to do with Mrs. Gantt. This unsatisfactory husband. . . ."

"Would hardly need to turn to murder. Besides, what reason could he have for killing the Rylands?" Anna pointed out.

"None, of course. Stupid of me. I'm not thinking very clearly this morning. Well. Well. I . . . suppose I must see to this gorgon of yours, this Mrs. Thynne. Her sudden arrival on the scene begins to look very suspicious indeed. Do you think she'd kill to save her school's reputation?"

"I honestly don't know, my lord. I don't think she would really consider me a danger. Even assuming that she knew my true identity, knowing my guardians she would probably believe—quite correctly—that I was merely being delivered to another prison. But whether she had anything to do with the murders or no, Mrs. Thynne is a most dangerous woman. Her appearance is everything that is genteel and respectable. She is considered a pillar of the community. It may well be that she will cause you to doubt my story. Oh, yes, she will. She'd have you doubt the evidence of your own senses with her smooth tongue. But I can prove who I am—as long as I am not locked away."

There were protests from every side, Lady Sarn's the loudest as she had the most practice in overriding any noise.

"Don't be silly, gel. If my grandson were so assinine as to try any such thing, he would be so hounded by Chloe and me that he would have to set you free in self-defense."

"I would call off the wedding," Chloe added cheerfully.

"I will be wary," Sarn promised. "You must remember I have Chloe's unhappy experience with the lady to harden my heart as well. Chloe, I think, means to stay and visit with Grandmama, so when I return to take her home, I will give you all a report on the interview."

The viscount hated to leave while the air still carried such heavy currents of tension and grief, but Chloe signaled him to go, that she could take care of Anna—Lady Annabelle, that is—so he did as he was told.

After Lord Sarn left, an expectant hush fell over the room, thick as snow, but Jesse neither spoke nor moved. Finally the old dowager, unable to bear the pain she saw in Anna's face, broke the silence.

"Come, Anna, you need a rest after so much excitement," the lively ninety-two-year-old decreed. "Chloe will sit with you until you fall asleep, and we'll be within call should you need us."

Lady Sarn and Chloe glared into the shadows and then left, escorting Anna to her chamber. They were followed by Oliver who expressed his disgust in a more vocal and profane manner. The doctor tried to give Jesse a chance to redeem himself but soon left, sarcastically prescribing a dose of salts for his host.

Some hours later when Lord Sarn returned, Jesse still hid in the shadows, but now he stood unmoving as marble outside the door to the room that had become the ladies' parlor since the arrival of Anna and the dowager. Chloe's light soprano and the dowager's piercing one could be heard laughing through the slightly open door. In order to cheer up the newly discovered heiress, they had encouraged Anna to reminisce about the happy days of her childhood, when her parents were still alive. Her rich contralto had lost much of the cold desperation that had colored her voice earlier, but not all. Although she recounted tales of the palace at Zschau and the royal court in Paris, her mind remained in the present.

Jesse knew it, heard the fear through the laughter, but felt powerless to help, had even lost the right to help.

He held a finger to his lips and led Lord Sarn away from the door, back to his male sanctum. Still in silence he poured them both a tot of brandy and quickly poured himself another, to his friend's disgust. Sarn had returned greatly troubled at heart, and the sight of Jesse's seemingly self-centered anguish touched a raw nerve.

"Feeling sorry for yourself? They say eavesdroppers hear no good of themselves. Did you get a rare earful upstairs? Damn you, Jesse, are you so self-righteous that you condemn a woman for lying to save her life—no, to save your damned life, yours and Noll's?"

"Is that what you think, Viv? That I blame her, can't forgive her? Do I really seem so petty? Oh, I admit I was . . . hurt . . . at first to think she had deceived me, betrayed our trust. I suppose she—they all—think I'm angry."

"Angry is hardly the word. You could have given some hint, for heaven's sake, said something. . . ."

"No, I couldn't! I froze. I'd never heard a firsthand account of hell before. The proper social response escapes me."

"You needn't shout at me because you made an ass of yourself."

"I need to shout at someone. If her guardians hadn't been killed already, I'd have gone and throttled the life out of them myself. There isn't a single expression of sympathy that doesn't sound utterly frivolous compared to what Anna has had to endure. And knowing her, we probably haven't heard the worst of it. No, I haven't anything to say. And the only thing I can do for her now is to help reestablish her in the world to which she was born—a world in which I can have no place."

"Now you are being worse than foolish. Why shouldn't Anna's world and yours be one and the same if you care for her?"

"Care? You know perfectly well I love her. I love her,"

Jesse repeated quietly, almost to himself, in a wondering tone of voice. "But it's not enough. The very first evening your grandmama came to stay she quizzed Anna unmercifully about her parents, etc. Anna said, with a look which hindsight reveals as no less than a smirk, that she did not think her parents and Lady Sarn moved in the same social circles. It was the truth. Your grandmother, although of excellent *ton* and a powerful force still in London society, could not aspire to being the intimate of all the royal courts of Europe—assuming the Corsican usurper had let them be. Anna knew Versailles the way I know your place and you mine. Her mother was a princess! Anna may joke how her father used to say Eastern Europe had no nobility, only royalty, but that is just the sort of joke one makes within the family. Not outside. And I am very much outside that world. You know it's true. Even county society thinks me virtually a hermit—a curmudgeonly one at that."

"That hasn't been Anna's world for a long time."

"I know that. And that's precisely why she must be returned to her birthright, her heritage, before she can make any other decisions about her life."

Lord Sarn thought about it for a minute. "I see what you mean. I don't agree with you, but I understand. But even if you mean to say good-bye forever, you need to make your peace with Anna first. She needs your help too much for you not to be upon terms."

Jesse was immediately alert. "Trouble?"

"You might say so. It seems entirely likely that the oh-so-respectable headmistress, Mrs. Julia Thynne, means to see Anna sent either to Bedlam or to the gallows. You see, Mrs. Thynne agrees that the Rylands falsely identified the dead girl as the heiress. She knows the Gallant heiress is alive—because she herself escorted the girl to Westerbrooke!"

chapter
XI

It was a somber quartet who traveled to the meeting Lord Sarn had scheduled with the solicitor Mr. Turnbull, Mrs. Julia Thynne, and her imposter. Anna's supporters were weeded down to the formidable dowager and Jesse Norwood. (Lord Sarn's presence was due primarily to his position as magistrate.) Those excluded took their rejection rather badly, fear having exacerbated everyone's nerves. Upon the receipt of the news of the existence of a pretender, Anna had uttered but one phrase, "So that's why," and retired immediately to her chamber. As Oliver and Lady Sarn were, for the time being, not speaking to Jesse, and Lord Sarn was obliged to escort his fiancée home, no further discussion on the matter had been possible. Now, although not a word had been spoken, the four travelers held but a single thought— that it was very likely that they were going to meet a murderess.

Since both Mrs. Thynne and the solicitor were already established in rooms at the Blue Boar, it was judged convenient to hold the meeting there. At such an early hour of the morning Mr. Huckaby counted it no trouble to reserve the taproom for the private use of the nobility, especially since his grace the duke took care to grease his palm generously.

Westerbrooke had come. As the heiress's intended, he might be reckoned an interested party. He had come prepared to welcome his bride with open arms and was naturally disconcerted to find two candidates for the honor. This put him in a most uncomfortable position, since to make advances to the wrong candidate could only cause the most devastating embarrassment. Worse, should the betrothal proceed further and the deception be discovered too late, he might find himself tied for life to a woman quite without fortune. At first glance the expensively gowned, pink and white miss, vouched for by the headmistress, seemed the obvious choice. Yet the more dowdy female, with no pretensions to beauty, had an air about her, an innate elegance. Despite the poverty of her attire, she had the respect and attention that servants give only to the real article. She had also acquired the support of the dowager Lady Sarn, a woman noted for her shrewdness and strict standards. The situation was most delicate indeed.

The duke therefore positioned himself very carefully at a point equidistant from both contestants where he could observe the proceedings without taking an active part in them. The solicitor, too, tried to preserve an impartial appearance, but as he honestly believed the fair young lady with Mrs. Thynne to be Lady Annabelle Gallant, his attempt was less than successful.

To Jesse, standing at Anna's elbow, her fear was palpable. But only those three who had come to know her spirit could sense this. To the others, the enemy, she presented a brave and confident front.

It was easier to understand the depth of Anna's fear now that the enemy was at hand. Mrs. Julia Thynne was a very formidable opponent—respectable, well-groomed according to her station, still handsome, even gracious. That her smile did not reach her eyes would be considered seemly reserve to most. The cold eyes reviewed her opponent's allies and paused, disconcerted but not dismayed.

The insipid blond who claimed to be Lady Annabelle Gallant gave a start of recognition when Anna entered the room, but quieted at a word from Mrs. Thynne. Her appearance seemed well-bred, but gave no indication of latent intelligence. Despite her claims, she was not a prime mover in the present affair.

Lord Sarn uncomfortably took charge of the meeting, coughing for attention. "Ladies and gentlemen. Let me say first of all that this is not a court of law designed to make any disposition of the inheritance of Lady Annabelle Gallant. We are here to inquire into the claims of these two ladies to that identity insofar as these claims may relate to the murder of the woman previously identified as the heiress, and the murders of Sir John and Lady Ryland. Should we be unable to disprove conclusively the claims of one or either, that will be a matter for the London civil courts to decide."

"My lord," the solicitor answered, "I am sure I speak for the ladies as well as myself when I offer our full cooperation in completing your investigation into the recent unpleasantness. I do not, however, see that there can be any question regarding her ladyship's identity." A gracious nod was directed toward the insipid blond. "Lady Annabelle has been known to me personally for four years. She comes under the chaperonage of her headmistress, a most respected lady, and was presented to me originally by her aunt and uncle."

"My aunt and uncle, if I may remind you, Mr. Turnbull, also confidently identified the murdered Mrs. Gantt as their niece. As their only purpose throughout their guardianship was to gain hold of as much of my inheritance as possible, their word in any matter concerning money must be considered less than worthless. Had I been allowed to meet you face to face, and reveal the nature of their conduct toward me, their days of unlimited credit would have been over. Even the likelihood of being blackmailed by their hired imposter seemed less costly, no doubt."

Anna's voice was cold, concise, and confident. Her shaft about the dishonesty of her guardians had hit home. Mr. Turnbull had questioned a number of the Rylands' dealings. But Mrs. Thynne had spread her own poisonous propaganda well. He gave Anna a pitying look and then ignored her.

"The girl truly believes her delusions. But you, my lord, must see that if Sir John and Lady Ryland had any ulterior motives, this gracious lady could not. The good name of a schoolmistress is her most precious possession. She could never risk her reputation by lending herself to so dishonest a scheme. No amount of money would be worth it."

"No amount? Not even the possibility of securing the entire Gallant fortune for her own daughter?" Anna asked, her eyebrows climbing skeptically.

Mrs. Thynne began to weep quietly and gracefully. She turned her tear-streaked handsome face upon the gentlemen. "Oh, Anna, how could you? My own sister's child. I tried so hard with her, my lord. She was like the child I never had. But she was always jealous of dear Belle. Refused to be satisfied with her lot in life. And then she started fantasizing, making up stories that she was really a princess—and turning the aunt who loved her into a villainess because I made her face reality. I was afraid when Belle's letters were stolen. But if . . . she can't be held responsible if she did . . . anything else. Have pity, my lord. These things are best handled in the family."

Jesse and Lord Sarn stared at Mrs. Thynne, fascinated as if watching the performance of a mesmerist, horrified by the realization that nine out of ten fools would be taken in by her act. She held all the cards, it seemed. Without proof. . . .

"Mrs. Thynne, do you have any physical evidence to support your claim that this young lady is your pupil, Lady Annabelle Gallant," Sarn asked, indicating the impervious blond, "and that this other young lady is your niece?" He gave Anna a comforting nod. So much for impartiality.

"Certainly I do, my lord. Mr. Turnbull has all the necessary documents relative to the case and can assure you as to their authenticity."

The lawyer handed Sarn a sheaf of official-looking papers. "I think you will find these all in order, my lord. If the other young lady has nothing to present for examination . . . ?"

"Not at the moment," Anna answered with a snap. "Naturally my mother's jewels are kept in a very safe place. Had I brought them with me to Westerbrooke, the thieves would have taken them.''

A hush fell over the room. The first crack in Mrs. Thynne's composure began to appear.

''The jewels of the royal house of Zschau were looted by the Parisian mob in the early days of the Terror,'' she gasped.

''Not at all. Mama was ever more practical, more realistic than my father. She realized when I was sent away that France had become very dangerous for people of our class. Perhaps she knew that Papa could not be dragged away before the crisis came. Anyway, she bade me take my most precious possession with me—a clock Uncle Louis had made with his own hands and given me for my birthday.''

Mrs. Thynne interrupted, less gracefully than before. ''An uncle who was a clockmaker! See, she condemns herself with her own words!'' The laugh that followed was just a little too harsh.

''Well, of course, the king was not really my uncle— although I believe there was some intermarriage between the Capets and my mother's family a century or so back. The clocks, naturally, were only a hobby. He was very clever with his hands.'' There was no boasting in Anna's tone. She was telling the simple truth, unaware how her memories of a kind old gentleman must sound to those who remembered or imagined the glory of the French court. ''So I got my clock and Mama gave me her jewels, all of them, and told me I must take them with me. That I must guard my inheritance as well as I could, but if there were . . . difficulties, Nanny might use them to see us home. But it never was necessary to sell them. I believe most of the pieces are famous enough to be immediately and definitively recognized. Jewels, unlike papers, cannot be forged.''

''I don't believe you. It's a trick—a trick to gain time.'' The mask slipped and the headmistress's rage and sudden fear showed through for just a moment before she regained control of herself.

Anna ignored her. ''My lord, Mr. Turnbull, is it safe to

assume that my possession of family jewels may be considered strong, if not irrefutable, evidence on my behalf?"

Sarn permitted a smile to sneak across his face, then covered it quickly. Mr. Turnbull looked as if he had been kicked in the stomach. As he looked into Anna's clear eyes, it occurred to him all at once that she might be telling the truth. If so, he had been the dupe of scoundrels for more than a dozen years.

"Yes, I . . . I believe it would indeed be safe to assume so. When . . ." His voice cracked. "When might you be able to present this evidence?"

Thinking quickly, Anna answered, "A fortnight should be sufficient time."

Mrs. Thynne recovered her voice. "Not that I credit it for one moment, but I suggest if the girl has something to show she tell the authorities—you, sir, or Lord Sarn—and that you acquire the evidence so that there can be no possible hint of foul play."

"Oh, that's rich. Do you take me for a fool, Mrs. Thynne? Evidently you have learned nothing about me in thirteen years but my true name. I have profited better from your 'tuition.' I've no intention of giving you a chance to steal the jewels first. Any 'foul play' will not be initiated by me."

"I don't understand, Mrs. Thynne," Lady Sarn interpolated in a dangerously silky tone. "If Anna were in truth your mad niece, how could you possibly fear that she might acquire jewels that disappeared years ago in France? You don't claim your protégée ever had them, so they could not be stolen from her. It is so difficult to keep one's lies consistent," she sympathized. "If only I could remember where I'd seen you before. Don't worry, it will come to me."

"Well, well, well." Mr. Turnbull had been reduced to flustered incoherence. "If there are no further questions, my lord . . . ?"

"Only to ascertain your movements on the day of Sir John and Lady Ryland's death."

"My movements . . . well, I don't remember exactly. I

was working most of the day on some papers in my chamber. I did step out once or twice—to get some snuff the first time, Spanish Bran, and later to take my evening meal in the common room below. I did not chance to meet the Rylands at any time. To be quite frank, I took special care that I should not, since they were in the habit of pestering me for funds.''

"Quite so. Mrs. Thynne?''

"Lady Annabelle and I did not arrive until quite late in the afternoon, as I am sure you are aware. Since we were quite fatigued from the journey, we took our beds immediately after a light repast.''

"Immediately? Without seeking any information?''

"I did question Mr. Huckaby about the curious and disturbing rumors which had reached us concerning Lady Annabelle's supposed demise.'' Mrs. Thynne was all gracious confusion as she continued. "He told us of the terrible attack on the coach, the lone survivor, the discovery of the villains' bodies. I confess that I didn't know what to think. Mr. Turnbull, the Rylands, his grace the duke, all would need to be contacted, but it seemed far better to wait for the morning and clearer heads.''

"You confirm all this?'' Lord Sarn asked Mrs. Thynne's protégée.

"I beg your pardon?'' The girl jumped, startled at being directly addressed.

"Lord Sarn wants to know what we did the night we arrived,'' Mrs. Thynne prompted.

"We had dinner in our rooms and went right to sleep,'' the girl answered by rote.

"Thank you. That will be all for now, then.''

The solicitor quickly scurried out of the room, but Mrs. Thynne tarried a moment, looking at the duke in a considering fashion. Might his support be won? Given his choice, surely he would prefer a bride like her protégée—pretty, fashionable, and not too clever. She had taken one step toward Westerbrooke when a rusty soprano stopped her in her tracks.

"The divine Julia is all the rage,
the daintiest morsel on the stage—
How lovely standing in a golden gown
and better still naked lying down.

The racing duke is under her sway
He knows a good mount, the sportsmen say
If you don't trust him,
Ask his coachman, Jim,
Or the groom who trots by Julia's side—
They all agree she's a wonderful ride!"

Lady Sarn grinned in delighted satisfaction to see her shaft hit home. "One of the advantages of living so long is that one remembers all the scandals everybody hopes were buried long ago. Knowing Ingold, he probably settled a decent sum on you, even if he strongly doubted the child's paternity. He's dead now, poor fool, but his eldest son was quite old enough to remember you."

"I don't know what you're talking about. And I'll thank you not to indulge your taste for barracks-room language in front of Lady Annabelle, and speak in a manner better suited to your age and station!"

"My dear Mrs. Thynne, a dowager viscountess of ninety-two years can say or do anything she damn well pleases. And I don't think Lady Annabelle was offended, were you, dear?" She turned to Anna with a wicked glint in her eyes.

"Truth is only offensive to the wicked. I'm not even surprised. Oh, don't forget your wrap, Caroline."

The blond girl turned automatically before she was pulled back in order by her mentor. They stalked majestically from the room.

Before Lady Sarn could be congratulated on her memory and her performance, Westerbrooke stepped forward, reminding the others of his presence. If the lawyer had not seen enough to decide, the duke had. To give him his due, the duke was probably unaware of the handsome picture he presented against the window, the bright rays of the noonday sun turning his hair and eyes to gold. Jesse took one look at the gilded duke—three inches taller and nearly ten years younger than he—and growled. His displeasure increased as the duke took Anna's hand and gazed into her eyes in a manner that could only be called sappy.

"Lady Annabelle, this is hardly the time to discuss the arrangements made in our behalf—and I shall certainly never press you on that matter. But I would like to offer my services. Anything I can do to help you regain your rightful position . . . well, I would consider it a great honor to be allowed to help." He kissed her hand with great élan, walked to the door and paused. "I don't suppose . . . you never received my letters, did you? Nor answered them?"

"No, your grace," Anna answered kindly. "My guardians could never have risked it. They would sooner hire someone to write the letters in a way that would be sure to appeal to you."

"Amorous popinjay," Jesse apostrophized the empty air after Westerbrooke left.

"Oh, I don't know," said Lady Sarn, still elevated by her recent success and feeling that Jesse deserved a little punishment. "I thought it was very gracefully done—neither too pushy nor too cautious. You know, my dear, you could do worse. I'd give him very careful consideration before you turn him off. You've heard us talk about his vices, but they're nothing out of the ordinary. And nothing you couldn't handle. And he has his virtues as well." The dowager indicated the scene outside the window where Westerbrooke could be seen conversing with his coachman. The two bore a striking resemblance to one another. "It's not every man who sees to those relatives who have no legal claim upon him. And his father was such an active man."

Anna gave the dowager an impulsive hug. "Mrs. Thynne was right. You have a wicked tongue and an evil mind. And I love you."

"Don't encourage her, Miss . . . *Lady* Annabelle. There'll be no living with her," the dowager's grandson pleaded. "So, tell us, what now?"

"Not here," Jesse commanded, stopping Anna before

she opened her mouth. "In private. And, as you'll have to tell the others too, you might as well only say it once."

An hour later, as they were all cosily gathered in the drawing room at Norwood Hall, Jesse was once again the voice of caution.

"This doesn't mean we've won. Oh yes, Lady Sarn has managed to cast considerable suspicion on Mrs. Julia Thynne's character. But the fact still remains that the Rylands presented that other girl to the lawyer as the heiress."

"If only they'd been intelligent enough to stay alive," Lady Sarn mourned. "It's so difficult to disparage the dead properly."

"Exactly. So the burden of proof still lies with Anna—Lady Annabelle, that is. . . ."

"Oh, please, I've been Anna for so long now. . . ."

"And that means that Mrs. Thynne has to kill Lady Annabelle before she is able to bring forth her proof," continued Jesse, ignoring Anna's protest. He looked around the room. "Is there anyone who doubts that Mrs. Thynne will try to do precisely that—and as soon as possible?"

"No, not yet," Anna answered surprisingly. She looked for some sign of emotion—warmth or distaste—in Jesse's eyes, but he had his features well under control. She might have been a total stranger to him. Anna carefully kept her own voice cool and continued. "Not until she can get the jewels. Didn't you see her face when I mentioned them? She lusts for them—even if she can never wear them or even admit to having them. A nabob's fortune, a marquess's estate, a princess's dowry—it's not enough. Julia Thynne has to have it all. So she will try to beat me, or follow me, to the jewels. Only then will she try to kill me."

"You take it pretty calmly, miss," the doctor commented.

"I don't take it calmly at all. I realize, better than any of you, to what depths of infamy Julia Thynne is capable of sinking. She's already got away with multiple murder. But if I am to prevent her succeeding with mine, I cannot spare the time or energy to indulge in hysterics. I must plan, and plan carefully."

"Robert doesn't know how to handle health," Lady Sarn explained. "If you would only swoon or have a fit of the vapors, then he would know how to help you!"

"We all want to help," the viscount added. "But we need to consider how that may best be done. I can't toss Mrs. Thynne in the roundhouse, more's the pity."

"It wouldn't serve any purpose. I'm sure she has more hirelings at her command. You'd only give her an undisputed alibi."

"Anna, you said she would try to follow or beat you to the jewels. Could she? Does she know where they are?" Oliver asked.

"No, but the choice of locations is so limited that she could come up with a good guess as to the general area. She knows quite well that there is no place I might have hidden anything at the school. Therefore I must have disposed of the jewels before I came to her academy. From the time I landed in England I only stayed in two places—the family seat which is near Folkstone, and the Gallant town house in London. As my aunt and uncle took over the town house for their own use, she might well reason that had anything been hidden there, my guardians would certainly have discovered it long since. Which leaves us with the Castle."

"And if she gets to the Castle first, she might find the jewels before we get there," Oliver reasoned in a worried tone.

"No," Anna consoled him, smiling. "She won't find anything but cobwebs at the Castle, knowing how my guardians took care of the place. But it brings her far too close for comfort. Julia Thynne doesn't really have to find the jewels. What she must do is find *me*—after I've recovered the jewels, but before I can bring them back."

"So what we need to figure out is how we can lead her, and her minions, astray," Jesse summed up.

"If Anna stayed here, you and I could recover the jewels for her," Sarn suggested to Jesse.

"No!" Jesse and Anna cried at the same time.

"Don't you trust us, Anna?" Sarn asked.

"Of course I do. But I can't direct you to the right place.

You'd not only not find my cache, you might very well become dangerously lost yourself. Besides, this is my adventure, my murder. I won't be shuffled off to the side, to have nothing to do but worry, while you two have all the fun.''

"Anna'd be a sitting duck if we left her behind. In a way, by going herself, Anna guarantees her own safety, at least temporarily. But if she will not lead Mrs. Thynne to the jewels, there is no need to keep her alive any longer.''

"I wish you would stop speaking of me as if I were a child you'd just sent to the nursery.''

"Keep your temper, child," advised the dowager. "And let Chloe speak. She has an idea.''

Chloe blushed under their combined stares, but her voice was strong and confident. "What if Anna and I change places? No, hear me out." She held up her hand, forestalling her fiancé's complaint. "Mother and I were to return to London soon anyway. All we need to do is hurry our plans a bit. Mama's a sport; she'll play along. Anna, Lady Sarn, and Viv come with us. When we reach London, Anna will go home with Mama, taking my place. And I'll go with Lady Sarn. The next day, while Lady Sarn and I go to the Gallant town house, hopefully followed, Anna can sneak away to the coast. It won't really be taking you much out of your way.''

"Anna can sneak away while you and Grandmama are being attacked by a murderess, you mean." Lord Sarn didn't like the idea much.

"Not if you do your part properly. Naturally I expect you to go to Bow Street and see that we are well-protected, and that the malefactor is immediately turned over to the law.''

"Well done, Chloe! I'm so glad someone with brains is marrying into the family. Don't look so pop-eyed, boy. We'll do fine, Chloe and I. You can be there yourself—in hiding, of course. And I'm not unarmed." The dowager pulled a delicate-looking firepiece with mother-of-pearl handles from her bulging reticule and waved it about negligently.

Her grandson buried his head in his arms. From this position his voice issued, despairingly. "And how does Anna then reach the coast—all alone?''

"Certainly not," Chloe and Lady Sarn answered in unison.

"I wouldn't dream of excluding any of us from playing a part. After Anna sneaks away from my house—disguised as a chambermaid perhaps—she can meet Jesse and Oliver and continue with her journey," Chloe continued.

"And what about me?" Doctor Abernathy asked. He had no intention of being left out either.

"There's always a chance that Chloe's diversion won't work. In that case, a secondary diversion at the Castle would be a good idea. John Coachman can give you extra support," Jesse decided.

"Well, now that that's settled, maybe we can all get some rest." Lady Sarn rose and kissed the girl good-bye, as if she were ready to retire.

"Wait a minute, my lady, all of you. Nothing has been decided. Do you think that I will permit any more innocent people to put their lives at risk for my sake?"

"Do you think you can stop us?" Jesse asked pointedly.

Defeated, Anna sighed. "You are all quite insane."

chapter
XII

Early the next morning a nervous and excited party left Sarn for the long ride to London. The junior Lady Sarn had been confused and quite disgruntled to see her house party break up so abruptly, but she had been unable, despite considerable pressure, to prevent or delay the departure. Lady Potterby proved to be the sport her daughter claimed, but was nonetheless bemused by the sudden entrance of intrigue into her placid existence. She tended to watch Anna as if she expected the heiress to sprout golden wings any moment. Had Lady Potterby noticed the array of weapons Lord Sarn considered necessary to have close by, her eyes would have grown even wider. Anna's warnings had not gone unheeded, and as a result the ancient traveling barouche carried a small arsenal. Anna noted the amount of precaution taken and was glad on two scores—not only were the ladies well-protected, but also the obvious nature of the protective measures would indicate to any followers what direction to take.

After all the fears and warnings, the carriage ride proved uneventful. Damp sheets and undercooked mutton were the worst dangers to attend their journey. That there would be grave dangers ahead no one doubted. What troubled Anna most, despite all of Sarn's measures, was that, safe or harmed, she would not learn the resolution of all their strategems until all were reunited again. If Anna survived, too, of course.

Only two days after departing Norwood village, Chloe and her mother arrived home—except that it was Anna, carefully hidden in a large, most fashionable bonnet, who entered the Potterby house with Lady Potterby. Lord Sarn, egged on by his fiancée, treated any watchers to a farewell scene of a tenderness and romance to rival Romeo and Juliet's. (And which gave Anna a fit of the giggles once the door closed behind her.) At the Sarn residence it was Chloe, dowdy for the first time in her life, her pretty curls flattened, who meekly assisted the dowager from the coach and into the house.

On the following day after their arrival in London, it was the still drab, governessy Chloe who, with the open aid of Lady Sarn and the hidden assistance of the viscount, braved the dangers of Gallant House. Only a few streets away, Lady Potterby's other daughters (all seven of them) made up a family shopping party to the Pantheon Bazaar, with a maid and footman in attendance. The maid was terribly stupid and complained of blisters. She was soon sent home.

Instead of returning to the Potterby residence, Anna made a few swift adjustments to her costume and repaired to a small coaching inn nearby where she was met, with no little relief, by Jesse and Oliver Norwood.

It was a clear measure of the shared sense of fear and urgency that such a breach of the rules of propriety was permitted. Lady Sarn, to be sure, entertained some hope that the enforced intimacy of the journey should reconcile all of Anna's and Jesse's differences. On the whole, however, the entire group was so completely focused on restoring Anna's fortune and the danger involved in doing so, that it was as if they had entered another world where the polite forms of social etiquette had no relevance.

Jesse, had his mind turned to such matters, would probably have said that the Gallant fortune would excuse any impropriety. As he had not yet made his peace with Anna, however, doing so was of major import. And as soon as he could discover a way to accomplish this end, he would change places with Oliver and let the boy drive the coach.

Oliver understood this now but was still annoyed on Anna's behalf. It must be admitted, however, that his overriding emotion was one of sheer pleasure at taking part in a real adventure, as chivalrous an episode as those in days of yore. In this year of our Lord 1805, a youth rarely found the opportunity to rescue a damsel in distress. Ever since the day when Anna had collapsed in their doorway, Oliver had felt that Providence had sent her to Norwood with a very definite plan in mind. True, part of the plan seemed temporarily to have gone awry, but that it would eventually straighten itself out Oliver had no doubt.

"I will never understand this joyful anticipation of physical violence that gentlemen so delight in," Anna said. "My father was just the same. He was actually looking forward to a good scrap against the jacquerie."

"I don't enjoy fighting."

"No?"

"No. I just . . . we just want to see the criminals apprehended so you'll be safe, that's all. We are just willing to use physical force if necessary."

"Your palms are itching, Oliver."

"Don't be ridiculous. I could never hit a woman. And if neither of our diversions works, I'll never have the chance anyway." Despite his protestations, Oliver sounded distinctly woebegone at missing any of the action. "It could be all over already."

"I wish I could believe that. Mrs. Thynne might have sent a lackey to London, simply because she doesn't take chances, but she is too clever not to expect some sort of funny business. I have too many allies for her not to be alerted to danger."

"Well, Doctor Abernathy and John are to meet us at Maidstone. We'd have liked to have pulled off the switch closer to the coast, but Maidstone is much the busiest town along this route. In the confusion, our changing places should pass unnoticed."

"Maybe we can plan a disguise for you for the way

back," Anna consoled. "We ought to have borrowed one of Lady Sarn's gowns for you."

"Not necessary, I assure you. Besides, I'm too tall and skinny for her clothes. Now Uncle Jess might. . . ."

Despite the ridiculous image conjured by Oliver's words, the mere mention of his uncle's name caused Anna's expression to darken. The youth was quick to sense her sorrow and his voice faltered.

"I never thought I'd say this about my uncle, but he can be the most egregious ass."

The corner of Anna's mouth twitched very slightly.

"Really, he is acting like an idiot. I know I told you how he's Valiant for Truth, but even he's not such a moralistic prude to blame you for protecting your life, and ours, by hiding a few facts. Oh no, he's just too much of an ass to tell you so."

Anna smiled at the aggrieved expression on the boy's face. "It doesn't matter, Oliver. I know Jesse has forgiven my little lies, despite his obstinate silence. What he can neither forgive nor forget is all that money."

Oliver could think of no answer to this.

In Maidstone the adventurers headed for the town's busiest coaching house, timing their arrival to coincide with that of the London stage. Amid the to-and-fro of the stage traffic, the trio made their way to the private parlor in the rear of the old inn virtually unnoticed. Or so they hoped. Three fellow conspirators, rather than the two they expected, already awaited them.

"Mrs. Mattingly! Whatever are you doing here? Oh, my dear, you shouldn't have come. It's far too dangerous!" Anna cried.

"Dangerous? How could a visit to my third cousin, twice removed, be at all dangerous? Poor Alf, he never did harm to a living thing in his whole life. Simple, you understand." The farmer's wife tapped her brow significantly.

"I understand too well. Does Mr. M. know what you've done?"

"Don't look at me like that, Miss Anna. You'll give

yourself wrinkles afore your time. Of course he knows. Drew lots, we did, all of us at the farm and the house. And I won. Terrible disappointed Sophronia Lucy was, but there it is.''

"You are incorrigible!"

"Am I now?" Mrs. Mattingly answered with a great smile. "In-cor-ri-gi-ble. I must remember to tell Mr. M. He says much the same, I dessay, but not half so grand. Incorrigible.''

"Now, miss, you're not to worry," the diffident groom said. "We're agreed Mrs. M. shall go no farther. And Cousin Alf is real enough. He'll be good cover for your trip to the coast. For he shall take you to his cottage and send you on from there."

"Come, deary," the farmer's wife said in a no-nonsense tone. "You shall have a good lie-down first. Then we'll have a real nice supper before you put on your disguises and be off. The food's quite good here, for an inn. Cousin Meg always had a light hand with pastry. Although my cakes are better, if I do say so myself.''

Following meekly out the door, Anna asked, "Another cousin?"

Mrs. Mattingly's answer was lost behind solid oak, drifting away into a comforting murmur.

"Mrs. M. will take good care of her," said John.

"Yes, she's a good soul. And a clever one. I take it our heiress now undergoes yet a third transformation into farmer's wife.''

"That's it, sir. I'm afraid it won't be a very comfortable ride for you and Master Oliver, though. You'll have to hide among the supplies and boxes we load on the trap.''

"As if it mattered. Have you checked out the stables yet?''

"No, sir. I was just about to do that now.''

"Do that, John. And see if the ostlers have noticed anyone who might be following us. Discreetly.''

"Do you really think you could have been followed?" the doctor asked after the groom had gone.

"I don't know, but I don't think we can take any chances.

Mrs. Thynne has proved her cunning and ruthlessness. Her very life is at stake now. Our success in foiling her plans may, in the end, be reduced to simple numerical advantage— that Anna has more friends than Mrs. Thynne has hired lackeys,'' Jesse said.

"How is Miss Anna taking all this? She looked a bit frazzled.''

Jesse shrugged. "Oh, you know Anna. She doesn't say much.''

His nephew regarded him with revulsion. "Oh, Anna's fine. She can't help thinking all her friends may be killed on her behalf. One of her friends won't speak to her at all. But she's just fine.''

"Not speaking . . . ?''

"Oliver evidently thinks I should be capable of driving a closed carriage and chatting with the passengers at the same time.'' Jesse's voice clearly forbade any further comment. "We're all a bit tense. I think it would almost be easier to have a more direct source of danger to face and overcome. It would be a great relief to bash somebody's face in. Well, come on, let's go over our plans.''

"Again?'' Oliver groaned.

If the two parties of adventurers needed some comic relief from tension, the sight of John Coachman dressed as Anna, and Anna as Mrs. Mattingly, certainly provided it. Doctor Abernathy could hardly keep a straight face while assisting "Lady Annabelle'' into the coach, and only the noise coming from a crate of chickens kept Jesse and Oliver from revealing their position.

Cousin Alf did not understand what was going on at all, but he was an obliging fellow who would not dream of disobeying any order of Mrs. Mattingly. Although simple, Alf had a special knowledge of his own that included a great affinity for the land and the animals that lived off it. He would be able to show Jesse hidden trails leading to the coast and to provide fresh mounts on the return trip.

A carriage was too lumbersome, too slow for further use. Its main advantage so far had been its disguising properties, the ability to carry passengers hidden, unseen. Once the jewels had been recovered, however, speed would be the primary concern. There would be no more stopping at inns for food or rest either. The main roads and the comforts offered along their routes would be avoided.

Mrs. Mattingly had seen that enough supplies and nourishment for a week's travel had been provided. The one thing the conspirators had forgotten was that Anna had not ridden a horse in thirteen years.

"I'm sure I shall do quite well. It's bound to come back to me, don't you think?"

"Damn. Of course it would come back to you. You simply won't be able to walk for a week."

"There isn't a sidesaddle either," Oliver noticed.

"All right then," Jesse said after a moment's contemplation, "up with you, Anna. We'll take the third mount along to give one of the others a rest. Better to save your muscles and ride pillion with me."

"Won't it slow you down?"

"Not as much as having you temporarily crippled would. Come on, up with you."

Anna mounted, hesitant but obedient.

"Well, hold on tight then," Jesse ordered brusquely. But when Anna's arms tentatively circled his waist, he took her hand and kissed it in silent apology before setting off.

For one silent moment Anna rested her cheek against Jesse's broad shoulders. If a few tears fell then, they fell unnoticed. Anna smiled as they trickled down her cheek.

The pace Jesse set now was hard and fast. Anna was soon glad that she had no more to do than hold tight. Their route, avoiding main roads and turnpikes, was often treacherous and demanded the skill of an experienced horseman.

They stopped only once, to rest and feed the horses as much as to rest and fortify themselves. Exhaustion kept conversation to a minimum, but Oliver noticed that the barrier between his uncle and Anna seemed mysteriously to have been lifted.

They rode through the night and as the new day dawned, the salt tang of sea air could be sensed in the cold breeze.

"According to Cousin Alf's directions, this path should lead us to shore some five miles south of Folkestone. An old smugglers' route, I suppose. You'll have to start guiding us soon, Anna."

"I only hope landmarks have not changed much since I was last here. And that we don't meet any real smugglers while we search. What we need to find out now is the time of high and low tide."

"Dare we stop at an inn so close to the Castle?" Oliver asked.

"Not at an inn, but perhaps one of us—alone—might stop at one of the fishermen's cottages."

"Be careful they don't take you for a Customs official."

Jesse rubbed his unshaven jaw ruefully. "An escapee from debtors' prison would be more likely. As soon as we can find a safe place for you to wait, I'll see what I can find out."

A tall hill soon gave them their first sight of the Channel— and of the Castle.

"Great Zeus!" Oliver's jaw fell open.

The fortress of the lords of Ware was built to inspire awe—and fear. It was meant to repel invaders first and house a family only secondarily. By no stretch of Gothic imagination could it be considered romantic. Ware Castle would make an excellent prison.

"Yes, remarkably well preserved, isn't it? If a trifle off-putting. I can't entirely blame my guardians for failing to find tenants. There's something about the place that always makes guests check their weapons and their consciences. I don't know why."

"I hadn't realized we were so close." Jesse also regarded the fortress warily.

"Oh yes. Only an energetic walk away."

Jesse's answer was no more than a grunt.

Shortly thereafter, Anna and Oliver crouched hidden among the bushes and rocks overlooking the Channel, while Jesse, with utmost caution, searched for a likely source of information.

"To think France is just a few miles across the Channel.

My father made the Grand Tour when he was my age. I wonder if I'll ever have the chance.''

"You will. It may take some time yet, but you will. It will be a very different world from the one your father saw, though.''

"Do you want to go back at all, Anna, when the war is over?"

"To France? I don't know. To Zschau, to my mother's home, yes, definitely. The only family I have left in the world would be there. If Napoleon does not destroy them as well.''

"You have family here. You have me and Jesse. And Lady Sarn, Viv and Chloe, Doctor Abernathy. . . .''

"True. And one's adopted family is usually so much nicer than one's relatives by birth." Anna cocked her head. "Did you hear anything?"

"Just the wind. And the birds. You're too nervous. Jesse can't be back for a bit yet.''

"I suppose. But we'd best keep our voices down. I wish we could see better from this position.''

"We daren't move. How would Jesse find us? Besides, we'd hear an approach even if we couldn't see it. Tell me, do you know this area well?''

"Not of my own knowledge, but through my father's eyes, yes. I never lived at the Castle for any period of time. But this is where Papa grew up. He knew every inlet, cave, and smuggler's haunt all along this coast. Knew the smugglers rather too well—that's why he was hurried off to India. But those friendships stood him well when he needed to send me home. One couldn't book passage on the Calais-Dover packet anymore.''

"So you came back on a smuggler's boat? What fun! And you hid the jewels in the smuggler's lair?''

"Not exactly.''

"Well, where did you hide them?''

"Yes, Miss Herries, where did you hide them?'' A deep, rough voice cried from behind them, causing both Anna and Oliver to jump, startled.

"Damn. I'm sorry, Anna. I should have listened to you.''

"It's all right, Oliver. We couldn't have run for it without being seen."

A giant, burly fellow whose rather natty clothes had become unkempt through exertion stood over Anna and Oliver. Two others stood some distance away. All three held weapons pointed at their quarry.

"Tie 'em up. We'll take no chances."

"Where's the other one?" a nervous, beady-eyed fellow asked while binding Anna's hands.

"Gone to the Castle, most likely. To lead us astray. Well, he'll meet a fine reception committee there." The thought amused the three villains immensely.

"Heavens, Mrs. Thynne's school must be quite depopulated. Is the entire staff looking for me?" Anna kept her voice under strict control, her eyes calm, staring at the incoming tide.

"Aye, but it's me that found you and me who'll get the reward. Now, you can tell me where the jewels are, or you can watch while I fill the young master here full of buck-shot. Which will it be?"

"Don't tell him, Anna. Once he knows where the jewels are he'll have no reason to keep us alive."

A swift fist to Oliver's jaw was the giant's response. "I've no reason to keep you alive at all, boy, so shut your mouth. Now, wot's it to be, miss? Shall I hit him again?"

"No! No, don't hit him. I'll tell you."

"Anna!"

"It's no use, Oliver. The jewels are in one of the caves along this cliff," she told her captors, hanging her head in defeat.

"That's better then. All right, now we go for a nice little walk. You lead."

There was a path down to the shore some feet away, steep but accessible, at least to those dressed for rugged climbing. Anna was not. When she had reached the last turn of the path, her feet lost their purchase and slipped from under her. Scrambling for some kind of hold, Anna tumbled the last few feet to the bottom of the hill.

"Get up now and lead the way."

"I can't . . . my ankle. . . ."

"Too bad. Get up or more than your ankle will be broken." To prove this was no meaningless threat, the burly leader of the trio boxed her ears with enough force to leave her dizzy.

Oliver, raised on tales of chivalry, could bear no more. Bound as he was, he butted into Anna's attacker and knocked him down. Having no weapon available but his feet, he used those to kick at the man's ribs. The effort was not only useless, but also foolish. The third villain simply pulled forth his pistol and shot Oliver cleanly through the fleshy part of his upper arm.

"Oliver!"

"I've been shot," he said stupidly.

"Yes, dear, but you'll be all right." Anna turned a threatening gaze upon her captors. "Either you allow me to bind his wound up, or I'll not take another step."

There was no doubt she meant it.

"Quickly then." The silent one unbound her hands and even helped cut away part of her petticoats to make a bandage. But the villains laughed to themselves, thinking how pointless an exercise it was. What did it matter if the boy bled to death or was drowned at sea?

"All right, on we go. How much farther?"

"Not far."

Not far, but difficult underfoot. Anna and Oliver practically had to be carried due to their injuries. Finally Anna collapsed to the gravelly sand.

"I can't. I can't go any farther. Here's the entrance. You've got what you want, just leave us!"

"Oh no, miss. Not until those jools are here in my hand." Moving aside a few rocks and bushes, the leader stepped into the cave opening. " 'Ere. 'Ow far does this go back?"

Anna shook her head. Her voice was barely controlled. In another moment she would be in tears. "I was a child when I was here last. It seemed quite far to me then. If you keep feeling along the right wall of the cave until you find a ledge, about chest height, that's where the jewels are."

Her posture was one of failure and defeat, but she gave

Oliver's hand a warning squeeze that held quite another meaning.

"Do we kill them now?" The beady-eyed one was in a hurry.

"No. Not until the jools are in our hands. Them's orders." He bent down and grabbed Anna's arm and twisted it, painfully. "You had better be tellin' the truth. Wat here is a trifle nervous, see? He might just kill you by accident if you were to startle him. So be good while we find the booty."

"Why not take 'em with us?"

"You want to carry 'em, go ahead."

"All right, all right. Give us a match."

Soon Anna and Oliver were alone with the nervous one called Wat, the only sound the waves of the incoming tide lapping closer and closer. Anna watched the waves anxiously. Suddenly Oliver understood.

"Do you mean you're actually going to hand those jewels over to Mrs. Thynne?" he asked.

Wat jumped. "Of course. That's what we was paid to do."

"Paid what? One hundred pounds to hand over a fortune worth over a million? You may believe that, but I'll bet the others don't."

"And what would I do with a million pounds worth of jools? Take 'em to a pawn shop?"

"Make Mrs. Thynne pay you what they're worth. If she's to claim my estate, she can afford it. She must," Anna added.

"I can't believe that other fellow hasn't thought of it already. Oh, I suppose he doesn't want to split three ways."

"Of course. All he has to do is tell Wat here that he never found the jewels at all. Wat is here. He'll never know."

Wat looked them over carefully—one with a twisted ankle, the other with a bullet wound in his arm. Where could they run to? How far could they get? Still, best to be sure.

"I suppose it won't do a bit of harm to check on our mutual investment. But you're not going anywhere while I do." He shredded the last remnants of Anna's petticoat to make another rope and tied Anna and Oliver together, back to back. "Ta, dearies. See you soon."

As soon as Wat had disappeared into the cave, Anna and Oliver began to struggle with their bonds.

"We've not much time, Noll. We have to get to higher ground."

"Thank God, they're all landlubbers. Can't tie a decent knot."

"I never thought I should be thankful for the pathetic state of my wardrobe, but it now seems the greatest good fortune that my petticoat is worn to shreds. Be careful of your arm, Noll."

"There it goes. I'll be all right," he insisted manfully, "but what about your leg? It's a rough climb."

"Oh I fell on purpose. My ankle is fine, though I did skin my knee. I'm fine. Let's go!"

There was no time to run back to the path. Water lapped about their ankles as they scrambled to the top of the embankment. Anna's hands were raw, and Oliver's arm had begun to bleed again, but they were safe.

chapter XIII

Exhausted and unable to move, Anna and Oliver lay on the grassy embankment. There Jesse found them some little time later.

"I've been out of my mind with worry. The fisher-folk were full of talk of strangers lurking about the shore and around the Castle. Are you all right?"

An immense feeling of peace descended on Anna as she saw Jesse and realized he was safe, unharmed. "We ran into a little difficulty," she answered with customary understatement. "But we seem to have outsmarted our pursuers. Oliver is going to need some medical attention, though."

"Will they be back?"

"No, they won't be back."

"Uncle Jess, you should have seen how clever Anna was! She...."

"Hush, boy. Let me look at your arm."

"Oh, go ahead. But you should have seen how brave Anna was, how cunning...."

"Oliver was very brave, too."

The boy flushed, but rattled on about their adventure while his uncle examined his wound.

"Well, that sounds very exciting," Jesse said depressingly.

The wound was clean, but the boy seemed likely to become feverish through sheer excitement.

"Jesse, what about Doctor Abernathy and John at the Castle? Our attackers mentioned there were more men stationed there."

"Weeelll, I think Robert and John may have some unexpected help. You see, I let it slip that the strangers were Customs men and that they'd heard some smugglers were actually hiding out at the Castle. They don't like Customs men hereabouts. You needn't stare. Did you think Anna was the only one who could be clever?"

"I think you're brilliant, Uncle Jess."

"I was even brilliant enough to get some candles for our foray into the bowels of the earth."

"True genius," Anna agreed.

At low tide Anna and Jesse entered the cave that had swallowed the three villains only hours before. Oliver, thankfully, remained outside, on guard.

"Anna, if the cave is underwater much of the time, how can your valuables still be safe?"

"Some of the cave is underwater at high tide, but not all of it. The greatest danger is simply getting lost. Some of the paths wind around the hills for miles and intertwine with others. We go to the left. You'll feel the incline."

"Yes, I can tell we're going uphill." The light from his candle revealed a few cases of French wine. "I hope all the smugglers have gone to the Castle to rescue Robert and John."

"We might find my father's name still a strong protection, even if we did meet some. These are the men who smuggled me out of France. Be careful now. The tunnel gets much smaller here."

"Small isn't the word. Anna, I don't think I can get through."

"Wait for me then. The cache should be just on the other side of this passage."

"Keep talking to me. I want to know you're not in trouble."

"I must confess, I was a good deal smaller myself the

last time I came through here." Anna's voice grew fainter as she crawled through the opening. "Blast. I'm fine, Jesse. My candle just went out. It's a good thing you gave me a flint box. There, I've got it! Now how am I to manage this and the candle through the passage?"

"Try pushing the treasure through first. My arms might just reach far enough—yes, yes, I have it. Lord, this is quite a haul!"

"Well, the clock takes up a good deal of space," Anna explained, her tousled head reappearing through the passage cavity.

"This place gives me the willies. Come on, lead us out."

"You missed all sorts of fun," Oliver told Anna and his uncle as they emerged squinting into the daylight. "Look, from up here you can see the Castle and the village. A whole band of villagers marched up to the Castle and chased another bunch of fellows down the road toward Hythe. The way they were running, they won't stop to breathe until they reach Eastbourne."

"Did you see Robert or John?" Jesse asked.

"I thought I saw John with the villagers, but not Doctor Abernathy."

"Come on, we're going to find him and leave you in his care."

"But, Uncle . . . !"

"You've played your part, and very well, but you can do no more until that wound heals. Whether you care to admit it or not, you need rest and medical attention."

"Oh, very well. But don't we get to see the loot?"

The small chest had no lock, a circumstance Anna had long considered fortunate. She could never have explained the possession of a key, any key, at Mrs. Thynne's Academy. Time and the elements, however, had caused the catch to stick and it took some little effort on Jesse's part before it could be pried open.

An elegant ormolu clock took up half the space in the chest. When it was wound, so Anna said, a funny little clown would ring the hours. More impressive to her audience was the inscription at the base of the clock—'*A ma chère Belle-Anne en honneur de son anniversair 10 aôut 1785, Louis XVI.''* In the other half of the chest, wrapped in velvet, jewels of all sizes and varieties spilled forth. The famous ruby parure was there, as well as incidental pieces acquired by the royal family over the centuries.

''What paltry things to risk one's life for,'' was Anna's sole reaction.

They decided that the Castle, having been rid of intruders so successfully, provided both the safest hiding place for the night and the most likely place to meet the doctor and John Coachman. Although uncared for in recent years, the Castle remained formidably elegant. The entire Georgian mass of Norwood Hall could be comfortably contained in the east wing alone.

Doctor Abernathy was still within, and John soon returned. They and Oliver settled themselves in the housekeeper's rooms in order to be close to the kitchens. Jesse camped uncomfortably in one of the salons, troubled more by unpleasant thoughts than by the undersized sofa. Where Anna went the gentlemen did not ask. After having endured so much male company the last few days, she deserved her privacy.

Anna walked the long gallery in silence, past portraits of the former Lords of Ware and their ladies. The title had died with her grandfather. Now she was all of Gallant blood that lived. And was it all to die now in her? Even if she saved her heritage from the rapacious greed of Mrs. Thynne, to whom would it go when the long years finally claimed their due? Anna knew herself too well to think that her love for Jesse could ever dim or change. There once was a time when she might have married for comfort or convenience, but not now. Was all their effort in the end to be for nothing? Was happiness still as far away as it had been in Mrs. Thynne's cold academy? Anna recalled Jesse's concerned face when he found them again on the cliff that afternoon. The memory provided no answers, however, only the reminder that other matters must be finished first.

The next morning Anna reappeared, looking refreshed

and calm. How dearly that calm cost her they would never know.

John had seen to it that she and Jesse had fresh mounts and provisions—the Lord only knew how. He would stay behind with the doctor to care for Oliver and bring him home in easy stages.

There was nothing easy about either the route taken or the pace set by Jesse. Following the advice of poor Cousin Alf, he again avoided the main roads entirely, cutting instead across fields and woods, down shallow frozen streams. Most of the heavy snowfalls had either missed this southern area or melted away. The wind still held a distinct bite. There was little cover for their passage. Trees and fields were bleakly naked of foliage. The occasional farmhouse or abandoned woodsman's hut was seen from a distance. Anna's and Jesse's costumes presented a prosperous farmer and his wife; their speed spoke more of an eloping pair of lovers fleeing a relentless father.

They rode through the night, stopping only to eat and to change horses. Eventually the strain was bound to tell. Jesse was used to an active life, but Anna was still frail from lack of care and illness. Near dawn Jesse became aware of Anna's weight heavy against his back, slipping more and more often.

"What are we stopping for?"

"We're stopping before you fall off. Come on." Jesse held out his arms to help her down. "Careful. Can you stand?"

"Yes."

"Liar." But this time it was almost an endearment. "Rest here a moment. It's almost light." He looked about anxiously. "I'd rather we stayed put until dark. The difficulty is finding a safe place to wait. A safe and warm place. Dare I leave you alone a few minutes while I reconnoiter?"

"I can. . . ."

"No, you can't. I can, of course, carry you over my shoulder. . . ."

"Don't even. . . ."

"No? In that case, let me help you up into this tree."

"Into the tree? I suppose if any attackers spot me, I disarm them by falling on top of them and thus render them senseless."

"That's right. But don't fall out otherwise."

"I'll do my best." Anna's assurance was a little shaky and her grasp on the tree trunk desperately tight. The loot-filled saddlebags Jesse temporarily buried beneath the next tree. Obviously Mrs. Thynne's hirelings had been carefully instructed to leave Anna unharmed until the jewels were actually in their murderous hands. Even if by some awful chance Anna were discovered, there would still be time for Jesse to run to the rescue.

Jesse would have liked a chance to run to the rescue, to be heroic, to have Anna watch him being brave and manly, thrashing any number of villains in her defense. Alas, this was not to be his grand opportunity. So unexciting had his absence been that Anna had fallen quietly asleep, still fiercely clutching her perch.

Taking care not to disturb her sleep, Jesse detached Anna from the tree and transferred her to his embrace on the tired horse, after he had recovered her treasure from the earth. A mile from the path, the ruins of an ancient monastery gave the winter landscape a stark dignity. Over the centuries villagers had carted away much of the stone for their own use, but there remained a quantity of unusable rubble and—which had pleased Jesse—a sizable portion of wall still upstanding. It was to that corner of the cloister that was still covered by a strong roof that Jesse carried the sleeping heiress. There he lay down with Anna held tightly in his arms and slept.

Hunger and the brightness of the midday sun finally woke the sleepers. Anna opened her eyes to find herself staring first at a comforting expanse of buff-clad, muscular shoulder, then up to find Jesse's warm brown eyes tenderly watching her. Beneath the slight stubble, his unshaven cheeks flushed warmly at being discovered. He made no effort to shift his position, however.

"I didn't dare light a fire. Are you quite warm enough?" he asked.

"Quite." Anna wondered what Jesse would do if she reminded him that this was not the first time she had slept in his arms. No, better not upset the precarious balance of their present relationship.

"Where are we, do you know?" she asked.

"Some miles north of Maidstone. We should make London tonight."

"Mmmmm." It was a prospect that Anna did not anticipate with any enthusiasm. Fear of the dangers that might still lie ahead paled before the realization that this moment was, in effect, Jesse's renunciation and farewell.

"Since you obviously have my itinerary all mapped out, tell me, what do I do when we reach London?"

Ignoring any implications beyond the immediate present, Jesse answered, "Lady Sarn has promised to bring the solicitor Turnbull to London and find an expert who can pronounce on the jewels. Once that's done you'll be permanently established." He gazed sorrowfully at her tense expression. "Be generous, Anna. You've given us so much. Let us do something in return."

"Even if it cost you your lives? Oliver could have died yesterday!"

"Would you have done less for any one of us?"

"But I owe you my life! If you hadn't. . . ."

"If you hadn't stumbled into our home, I'm quite sure you'd have made it either to the village or to Westerbrooke. It has been distressingly obvious to all of us who love you that you could have managed to save yourself, regain your fortune, and probably catch the murderers without any help whatsoever. You owe us nothing. It is you who have done all the giving."

"I? I didn't even give you the truth until it was forced out of me." Anna hung her head, one phrase ringing over and over in her ears through the enveloping mists of shame—"all of us who love you."

"Oh, but you did. You opened our eyes to so much that we had never seen or considered before. Not only to cruelty and greed the innocent heart never imagines, but to the strength of the human spirit in adversity and its generosity.

There's not one of us who's not a little wiser, a little kinder, more patient, and stronger than we were before you came into our lives. You brought grace to Norwood.'' He gave a wry grin, trying to gain control of his voice. ''A quality singularly lacking in our home for some time. Oliver's become a man before my eyes. Lady Sarn's had ten years taken off her age, probably the ten years you've frightened off my life span. Most likely you haven't even noticed how Chloe models herself after you, so that she will be a good viscountess to Sarn. You laugh? It's true. Even Viv, that worldly-wise nobleman, has grown somehow. He stands a little taller, walks more briskly. I don't know. . . .'' Jesse shrugged and focused his eyes on the bay mare as he continued. ''And as for myself . . . well, I've been turned upside down and shaken until my few remaining wits rattle around my brain like dice in a cup.''

''I'm sorry. I never meant to upset. . . .''

''Well, you did. Thank God! I was in grave danger of becoming a . . . a fossil. If it hadn't been for Oliver, I wouldn't have been alive at all. In my arrogant, superior fashion I had decided that ninety percent of the human race were fools or worse. I should have realized that I was the biggest fool of all. But you've taught me that one cannot resign one's commission in the human community short of death. I mean to do better from now on. Who knows? I may even stay in London long enough to see your triumphal entry into society.''

So there it was. Anna's eyes followed him while Jesse, in embarrassment and sorrow, finally disengaged himself from her embrace and moved about caring for the horses and gathering their remaining food together. And he thought he wasn't running away from life anymore! Folly indeed. Folly, most of all, to speak of love to one who had never dared hope before. With that one word he had changed Anna's whole world. Well, this was not the time to argue some sense into him. Anna had vowed to bring the murderers of Annabelle Gantt to justice and that had yet to be accomplished. But once that was done. . . .

chapter
XIV

By the time the sun slipped below the horizon, Anna and Jesse were well on their way toward London. This was the most dangerous leg of their journey. There was even less natural cover, and fewer isolated patches. Mrs. Thynne was bound to have spread her net around the city. Lady Sarn's town house might well be observed, and the solicitor had undoubtedly been followed. Jesse was therefore astonished to find himself and Anna, their safety unchallenged, being graciously led through the servants' quarters to Lady Sarn's boudoir.

The aged dowager, and her grandson when he was fetched, were full of questions, one following another with such rapidity that it was impossible to answer a single one. Then before the travelers could gather breath to properly greet their hosts, they were whisked away to bathe and change.

"Mind you, Viv," Jesse said from the steaming water of the hip bath, "I'm not denying I was in great need of a shave and a bath. But why the hurry?"

"Grandmama means for us to have the jewels appraised this very night. Where are they, by the by?"

"In the saddlebags—there. Wouldn't it be safer to wait for daylight?"

"Grandmama says, and she may well be right, that every

minute we wait gives Mrs. Thynne more time to plan and . . . Jupiter!'' Lord Sarn had peeked in one of the bags. ''What was I saying?''

''That waiting would only give. . . .''

''Oh yes. You may add to that the fact that every second these are in my protection I feel nervous as a cat. The sooner these are safely stowed elsewhere I'll feel much better. I don't even know if Grandmama's little wall safe is big enough to hold all of this.''

''I suppose she has a point. By the way, I take it you had no trouble at Anna's town house?''

''Grandmama thought it was very tame. Only three hoodlums—she could have taken them all on herself without the help of two Runners and me. Chloe enjoyed herself. I tell you, Jess, there are times when women frighten me.''

''Don't they just. What's the plan for tonight then?''

''I wish I knew. This is all Grandmama's doing. She won't even tell me all of it. But then I've not told her everything I've done. All I know is Anna's to sneak out through the party next door in yet another disguise. Where we go from there Grandmama refuses to say. There's half a dozen Runners protecting the house. Tonight they'll put on livery to act as Anna's footmen and outriders.''

Jesse didn't like it. There would easily be a full twenty minutes that Anna would be out of his sight, and, when she came out to the carriage, a good few minutes when she would be in full view of anyone who wished her ill. But perhaps Lady Sarn was right and the sheer bravura of her plan was its greatest guarantee of success.

Although town was very bare of company, Lord Humphries had managed to gather together enough friends, fellow politicos and their families for the most part, for his wife's annual thirty-fifth birthday celebration. Since town was also very bare of entertainment for those forced to endure the city during the winter months, the event enjoyed a certain popularity which in general the dull personalities of the host and hostess would fail to warrant. As a result, the road before the Humphries' house—and Sarn's—was thick with coaches waiting for the exit of their proprietors.

It was to a particularly large and resplendent barouche that Jesse, the dowager, and her grandson silently crept and entered, while an unruly team farther down the street provided a moment of distraction. Anna, escorted by one of the Runners, had walked across the dowager's garden, through a small gate into the Humphries' rose garden. On the terrace she slipped off the enveloping black cloak she wore and stepped into the ballroom.

Waiting nervously in the coach, Jesse almost didn't recognize the elegant vision in ermine and black velvet who came so confidently toward them. Damn it, she was actually wearing the rubies!

It was not until the coach was once again underway that the livid Jesse had time to notice that Anna was chaperoned by a well-bred spinster of indeterminate age, who was introduced to him as the Lady Euphemia Humphries.

"It was very kind of you to help us, Lady Euphemia," the viscount said warily. "I don't know how much my grandmother told you. . . ."

"Lady Sarn has been kind enough to take me fully into her confidence—a confidence you will not find misplaced. I am honored to have been allowed some small part in the princess's adventures."

Princess? Lud, she probably was!

"You do understand, Lady Euphemia, that there is some risk involved?"

"You mean that this wicked headmistress may attack the coach and try to murder us all? Yes, I am fully prepared for that eventuality. Although she would have to be very foolhardy indeed to attack this coach."

Why this coach in particular? Jesse wondered. He had another question, too. "Tell me, Lady Sarn, what would you have done if we hadn't arrived in time for tonight's ball?"

"Oh, we had any number of contingency plans, didn't we, Euphemia?"

"Certainly. When one has lived in court circles for as long as we have, one becomes quite adept at intrigue and strategy."

"Grandmama, where are we going?" Sarn asked, deeply suspicious.

"To have the jewels appraised, of course, silly boy. Be patient, we still have quite a way to go. And don't you look so panicked, Jesse Norwood. We've two outriders ahead and another two behind. Mrs. Thynne is not a fool. What do you think is going to happen?"

Even at this late hour, the roads were not devoid of traffic. Jesse and Lord Sarn kept a careful eye on the occasional horseman or carriage that passed by, but all continued on their way, quite innocently, without any change in pace.

The outriders maintained a comfortable distance from the coach, the better to give advance warning and to provide a flanking movement if necessary. Since the gentlemen standing guard at opposite coach windows could not see the ostlers from their vantage point, they were not immediately aware of the absence of their reassuring shadows. Nor could they be aware that their coach, without hesitation or change in tempo, had altered course from the direction only Lady Sarn and Lady Euphemia knew. Even when the coach finally halted, Jesse and Lord Sarn were cautious, but no more than that. The Runner who rode with the coachman and acted as guard assured the passengers that the problem was no more than a piece of rock caught in one of the horse's hooves.

"Let me have a look at it," Jesse suggested, as he was the authority on horseflesh. As he alit from the carriage and passed the Runner, he was struck a brutal blow that felled him.

Those inside heard no more than a dull thud as Jesse's body hit the ground. Anna was the first to realize how peculiar the silence was.

"The two Runners acting as rear guard—I don't hear them."

The dowager boldly stuck her head through the window. "You there, what's going on? Where is . . . ?"

Her question was answered by the pressure of cold steel against her temple and a sinister threat.

"Anybody moves and the old lady dies."

Only then did Mrs. Thynne and her hired ruffians come forth from behind the roadside hedge. She walked to the other side of the carriage, smiling and with an arrogantly pleased swing to her hips. Tonight the mask was off, and she looked just what she was—a nobleman's cast-off mistress, greedy and malicious.

"My compliments, m'lord, ladies. You did very well for a group of amateurs. Alas, but you forgot one thing— Runners can be bought. Most people can. Now, while Lady Sarn is otherwise occupied, I suggest the rest of the company exit by this door."

"Jesse! What have you done with Jesse?" Anna cried.

"Be still! He's not dead—yet. Leave him there. My gift to you—he'll never know what hit him."

"You'll never get away with it, you know. The outriders will realize something is wrong. They'll be back any moment now."

"I don't think so. By the time they realize they've been guarding the wrong coach for the last few miles, it will be far too late."

"There are too many people involved," Anna insisted. "At one time you might have disposed of me without question, yes. But you cannot decimate a sizable percentage of the nobility and expect no reprisal."

"Oh, I daresay the murderess will be convicted and hanged. Better than Bedlam, don't you think? But it will be the madwoman known as Anna Herries who will be condemned and hanged, not I. I am in London. There are witnesses who can swear to that."

"More people who can be bought?"

"Quite a number of the nobility are obligated to me, as you should know. The reputation of my school must remain untarnished, lest their reputations also suffer. No, I shall never be suspected. Why would I kill all your friends and leave you untouched?"

So that was her plan. How diabolically clever! "But I do not have the funds to buy assistance," Anna argued, her eyes taking careful stock of the situation. "You expect to make the authorities believe I overpowered four people, two of them particularly healthy male specimens?''

"The mad are notorious for their strength and cunning. Milord is obviously easily controlled by a pistol to the head of his grandmother, and no doubt the unconscious gentleman would be as well. Your carriage is so well armed, too. I give you leave to try and think of an explanation why you were left alive. Tell the truth, and they will surely think you mad.''

Lord Sarn, his grandmother, and her elderly friend were herded to the side of the road by one of the two henchmen who had accompanied Mrs. Thynne. The traitorous Runner had collected all the weapons, not forgetting even Lady Euphemia's hidden pistol and the stiletto strapped to Lord Sarn's leg, then mounted negligent guard over the recumbent Jesse, his pistol directed at the others. Off to the side Anna was watched by the evil headmistress herself. There was no help to be had from the coachman—he was either drugged or dead. The horses were held by the other lackey.

Was there a slight change in Jesse's position, or had fear made Anna delirious? If she could only keep Mrs. Thynne talking. . . .

"There are others who can swear to having seen the jewels, you know,'' Anna reminded her captor.

"The boy and the doctor? From what I hear of the baron, Lord Norwood will never allow his son to become any further involved in so distasteful an affair. A rumor that you had seduced the boy should do the trick. Your superannuated apothecary can be handled, too, one way or another. In any case, they can neither of them swear that the jewels they saw were in fact genuine. Believe me, there is not a circumstance that I have not considered, not one that I cannot deal with successfully. So bring me the jewels and say a last good-bye to these poor fools you call friends.''

On her way back to the coach, Anna stooped for a moment by Jesse's side, caressing his face lovingly in farewell. Her eyes filled with tears, then hardened. No matter what the cost, Anna would destroy Mrs. Thynne's plan. Jesse must not die, he must not. As if to seal this contract, Anna took Jesse's hand in hers only to have her comforting grasp returned. Could the others see it? No, her body shielded their hands from view. Perhaps all hope was not lost.

The clock Anna left in the carriage. Lady Sarn had provided her own traveling jewel case for the rest. Anna swiftly pulled all she could hold from the case, brilliants gleaming in the moonlight, dripping from her fists.

"You want my jewels? Here, take them!"

The jewels made glittering arcs across the sky as Anna strew them all over the grassy verge, some of them landing in the road, in a ditch, and hanging from the bushes like a festive decoration.

As a distraction, Anna's gesture was magnificent. So, too, was her aim. Far-flung bits of jewelry caught the greedy eyes of the guards as well. Mrs. Thynne, her mouth pouring forth a stream of obscenities, put aside her pistol to gather up with both hands the gems she had sought so diligently and mercilessly. It was just the opening Jesse had waited for. From his prone position, he reached out for the Runner's legs and pulled them out from under him.

In his upheaval, the Runner's gun went off, frightening the horses to the point that the guard in charge was completely occupied in calming the team. Sarn, who like Jesse had only been looking for the right opportunity to move, took advantage of a moment's abstraction on his guard's part and, with a swift kick, disarmed the henchman and fell on him. It took surprisingly little time before the three men were overcome and pinioned together.

Julia Thynne did not even look up from her task. So sure was she that her plan must succeed that it never occurred to her that her hired thugs might be overcome. On Lady Sarn's recommendation, the headmistress was allowed to finish her task. ("Let her do it. Why should we have to grub around in the dirt?") Mrs. Thynne looked up to face her own pistol, held in Anna's steady grasp. Sarn had volunteered to act as coachman, as their own proved to be drugged. He held the horses steady while the others regained their arsenal and surrounded the failed villainess.

For the first time in her life, Julia Thynne discovered what it was like to be thoroughly terrified. Her mind, unable to accept the idea of defeat, snapped.

"No, they're mine. I deserve them. Do you know how hard I worked for this? Stuck in some provincial backwater, when I was meant to shine in London. Caroline, too. Why, these are wasted on that plain, pasty-faced heiress. Caroline and I, we know how to wear these, how to use money, too. I won't give it up now, I won't."

The stream of insane abuse continued. Anna walked away from it in disgust and pity. It was left to the two elderly ladies to restrain the now pathetic murderess and remove Anna's treasure from her greedy hands.

The rest of the evening passed by like a strange dream to Anna. Having no other way to dispose of Mrs. Thynne, they placed the bound and gagged woman in the coach, along with the drugged coachman, to ride with the ladies, while Jesse and Lord Sarn took the driver's place. The three hired lackeys were tied to the coach rigging and forced to trot along smartly.

Once their destination was reached, the captives were efficiently taken in charge. An emotionally exhausted Anna and her supporters were led through an elegant corridor to a private room where an extremely ugly old lady was attended by the solicitor Turnbull, another gentleman, and a number of weary ladies-in-waiting.

Without prompting, Anna dropped to her deepest curtsey until the old lady bid her rise.

"Abigail is right, you do have a look of your mama. Come here, child. I have been looking forward to your so exciting story. And then we shall have a look at your jewels, yes? And these fine gentlemen will settle this matter legally."

Since the King's illness, London's social life revolved around Carlton House rather than the Queen's Lodge at Windsor, but dull and homely as she might be, Charlotte of Mecklinburg-Strelitz was still Queen of England—even if the King in his strange fancies sometimes denied it—and she still knew how to wield her influence when called upon. It was still to her that young debutantes must be officially presented, not her son's unofficial consorts. The fount of honor was still her husband and the father of her large family.

The unknown gentleman proved to be Mr. Rundell, of Rundell and Bridges, London's most prestigious jewelers and jewelers to the royal family. He went into ecstatic raptures over the stones, while the Queen gave the provenance of those pieces she could remember from her childhood visits to Zschau.

At last Anna was guaranteed her rightful place in society, her wealth and heritage restored. And all she could think of was her vow unaccomplished and her happiness in retreat.

chapter
XV

The sudden appearance upon the London scene of a fabulously wealthy, beautiful lady of impeccable birth and breeding was guaranteed to cause quite a stir. When one added to this a most romantic (if heavily edited) tale of imprisonment and danger, of a murderous attempt to steal the heiress's very name and heritage, the result was only to be expected. London, so bare of company just days before, was now so full that those of the upper class, and those that clung to its fringes, found suitable lodgings difficult to come by. Every fashionable hostess sought the heiress's attendance at her soirées; every handsome fortune hunter sought an introduction; every merchant sought her custom. Society found its new favorite utterly charming and witty, with a grace and style all her own. True, Lady Annabelle could sometimes give voice to the most eccentric thoughts, and she was also known to possess a somewhat bizarre sense of humor (she had fallen into a fit of the giggles once upon hearing her beauty praised in bad verse), but these small imperfections were excused by the unorthodoxy of her upbringing.

True to his word, Jesse remained in town to see Anna's triumph, miserable though it made him. His brother, Lord Norwood, amazed at the change in Oliver, had suggested the boy stay with him awhile and acquire a little town bronze while his wound healed. The baron did not quite know how to deal with this newfound confidence in the son who reminded him unhappily of his renegade wife, except for the clear directness of the boy's gaze that left the baron slightly uncomfortable.

Those who had shared in Anna's restoration to fortune also basked in the reflected glory of her popularity—an honor that alternately amused or annoyed them, but that was taken seriously by none. Lady Sarn at least derived a great deal of enjoyment from what she called "the circus."

But the dowager, as well as Oliver, realized something was wrong, something more than Jesse Norwood's aloofness. Anna, or Lady Annabelle as she was more properly called now, simply was not behaving like a woman who has had all of life's problems, except romantic ones, solved.

"Listen, Anna, you're not worried about having to give evidence or anything like that, are you?" Oliver asked. "Because Sarn says Mrs. Thynne may never live to stand trial. Evidently caught some dreadful fever from one of the other inmates. Or. . . . you're not feeling sorry for her?"

Oliver had the honor of being Lady Annabelle's escort for the afternoon while she visited the lending library and the shops. Since Anna enjoyed the walk most of all, the shops were merely an excuse for exercise.

"Sorry for Julia Thynne? No, she chose her own path. For her daughter, a little. Caroline really never learned any other way of life."

"I'd heard you'd provided a post for her."

"For what it's worth. She has—or will have—a good deal of her mother's money from the school, so how long she stays as a governess is questionable."

"You've done all you could. More. You can't let that girl's possible future disturb you."

"Oh, I'm not worried about Caroline. Stupid as she is, she always manages somehow to land on her feet, like a cat."

"Then why do you still worry as if the murderess and her gang hadn't been caught? You're safe now."

"Am I? But the murderers of Mrs. Gantt still haven't been caught."

* * *

"She said what?" Jesse shouted.

"Anna said Mrs. Thynne had murdered her aunt and uncle, and had hired men to kill her. But her hired killers were not the men who first attacked the coach and killed the woman with Anna."

Oliver had interrupted his uncle in the middle of his correspondence with Mr. Mattingly at the Home Farm.

"The two who died in the blizzard. . . ."

"Were probably outside help at the school—grooms perhaps. Anna thought they looked vaguely familiar, remember? Sir John and Lady Ryland might have seen them when Mrs. Thynne brought her daughter to town to masquerade as Lady Annabelle. Anyway, it seems probable that the Rylands recognized them and tried to blackmail Mrs. Thynne with the knowledge. But Anna's point is. . . ."

"That those two could not possibly be the two who shot her and killed the other woman, because the color of the eyes is wrong. And she remembers their eyes very clearly, tawny gold and opaque black."

"But two sets of voices," Oliver added.

"Damn! We've been so hard on the trail of the schoolmistress that we forgot. Except Anna cannot forget, and she will never rest until the murderers of that poor woman are found. So we're right back to where we started."

"Looking for a possible heir to one of Anna's three fortunes."

"It sounds fantastic," the Duke of Westerbrooke commented. "Quite like one of Mrs. Radcliffe's stories." The duke was ignoring Jesse's narrow-eyed glare with great determination. Until Lady Annabelle forcibly insisted on his removal, he intended to stay comfortably ensconced in Lady Sarn's favorite wing chair.

"Too much like one of her stories. I can hardly take such a possibility seriously—except that I am quite positive that the men who attacked my coach have not been caught."

"I can't think how they escaped the area. Our search was very thorough," said Jesse.

"Well, obviously they did get through." Westerbrooke enjoyed being able to needle his pompous neighbor.

"Not necessarily," Jesse responded. "What if they were local people? Faces so familiar nobody would connect them with the murder?"

"You're grasping at straws, Norwood."

"Aren't we all?" said Anna, her quiet tone restoring peace. "It seems to me that we are left with the assumption that either one of his grace's houseguests or one of the local people is actually the long-lost descendent of the third marquess's second cousin."

"What about your other two fortunes?" Jesse asked.

"I'm virtually certain my father's friend in India never knew he was in the will. Papa's lawyers insisted he name a residuary legatee since I was a minor, so he gave them the first name to pop into his head. Since I came into my mother's fortune—legally if not in fact—when I was twenty-one, those relatives would have to be very sure indeed that I had not already made a will, and only someone who knew the truth about Mrs. Thynne's school could know that."

"And your aunt and uncle covered their tracks too well for that, you think?"

"Oh yes. In fact, it's surprising the murderers weren't looking for Caroline Thynne, since she had masqueraded as me a number of times for the solicitor."

"Yes, since the murderers were in no doubt that they had stopped the correct coach, they must have known the truth about your situation," Westerbrooke reasoned.

"What about the Rylands? I know you discounted them before, but they alone could have known your travel plans—other than Mrs. Thynne, of course."

"Oh, I don't know. The duke might have known," said Anna in a pensive tone, only the glint in her eye indicating that she was not serious.

"I?" Westerbrooke vaulted from his seat in horror. "Surely you cannot seriously suspect that I would have the slightest motive for harming you, Lady Annabelle."

"Calm yourself, your grace. I spoke only in jest."

"But you do have a point," Jesse maliciously pointed

out. "Westerbrooke could have discussed your travel plans with another of his guests."

"I could have, but I did not. Besides, due to the severe weather conditions, there were a number of guests who might easily have been coming down the same road at the same time." The duke struggled to regain his composure. "This continued speculation is useless. My only concern, dear Lady Annabelle, is for your personal safety. And I fear, if your assumptions are correct, that danger will continue until you gain full control of your grandfather's fortune, when you are thirty or . . . when you marry."

Did the duke really mean to imply that Anna should marry him to save herself from murder? "I think Anna's safety may well be assured by advertising the fact that we are still seeking the murderer. Under such conditions all those whose lives were touched by the circumstances of the murder must be very careful indeed to avoid suspicion. Unless Anna threatens to marry, the murderer can afford to wait," Jesse said between clenched teeth.

"But not indefinitely. And Lady Annabelle need not advertise her intentions to wed beforehand. My dear lady, I beg you will consider my words carefully."

"Rest assured, gentlemen, I shall take no action without proper consideration of *all* the facts. And I shall not forget your kindness in stopping by and giving my little problems your attention, your grace. No doubt I will see you at Lady Potterby's later this week."

This was dismissal. The duke recognized it and accepted it gracefully. "I will look forward to seeing you there. And I will expect you to save a set of country dances for me. Our steps match so well, it is always a delight to dance with you."

"Our steps match so well," Jesse mimicked as soon as Westerbrooke had departed. He added a rude epithet.

"Yes, I thought I had better get rid of him before you resorted to violence."

"Has he been pestering you like this much?"

"The duke calls quite frequently." Anna discovered in herself an amused pleasure at Jesse's indignant jealousy. "He brings me poetry."

How low could the man sink? "He talks rubbish. If there is another attempt on your life, it's Westerbrooke I'll suspect of trying to frighten you into marrying him. It just occurred to me—he has the right color eyes to be the murderer."

"You only noticed that now? He's the right build, too. But the voice is not quite right. And, unfortunately, there are 150 people who can swear he was not marauding on the highroads at the time of the attack."

"Pity. You're right, of course. Murder is much too energetic a crime for a fop like that. Poetry!"

"Bad poetry at that."

"Then why do you tolerate him? You don't. . . ." Jesse experienced a horrible moment of doubt. "You can't take him seriously, can you?"

Another woman might have taken advantage of a loved one's jealous suspicions. The thought did not even occur to Anna. "Do you think I have suddenly become a fool, Jesse? You're hardly flattering. Of course I don't take him seriously! But I've discovered that one of the penalties of wealth is that it attracts all manner of fools. Westerbrooke is no worse, and a good deal better, than the other fortune hunters who pursue me. And I owe him some courtesy, after all. He had no reason to think I would be unwilling to marry him."

"You didn't believe that story of his about falling in love via the post?"

"Certainly not. My guardians would never have gone to such trouble. The duke has a pathetic desire to appear well to others, and will say anything to achieve that result. But even if he were himself involved in blackmailing my guardians into promoting the match, he still never had a hint that I would be averse to a marriage of convenience. He proceeded with the wedding plans—at some cost in time, trouble, and money—all in good faith. It hardly seems proper to tell him now he's served his purpose, he can be off."

"You think he'll find it easier being refused on his own merit?"

"I think I can manage to couch his rejection in such terms as will leave the duke's tender self-esteem undamaged." *I will tell him that I fell in love with you before ever I met him. One cannot be offended by acts of God,* she thought.

"I hate to admit it, but I do think he may be right on one point. Once you are wed you will be safe." Only the tension in his clenched fingers revealed how much such an admission cost him.

Anna raised her eyes hopefully. If Jesse were to offer, even if only to save her life, she would not be too proud to accept. If he were not such a proud fool himself, he would see that they belonged together.

"Surely some of your suitors are neither fools nor fortune hunters?"

Discouraged, Anna raised a skeptical eyebrow. "There are at least three who have *not* written a sonnet to my left eyebrow. The duke is one of them. I have fought too hard for my heritage, however, to hand it over to a husband I married only for physical safety. You know, it's quite strange. I *know* the murderers are still at large, yet I don't feel personally at risk. I can't make myself feel afraid."

"Well, I am afraid. I don't know which worries me more—what the murderer might do, or what you might."

"On that score you may put your mind at ease. I simply can't think of anything to do. I haven't any direction to explore. I haven't even been very successful in the small chore I set myself—finding Mrs. Gantt's family to inform them of her death."

"You hadn't much information to go on."

"No, but you'd think by now someone would be searching for news of her. And certainly the story of the attack on the coach has been well publicized. Since my claim was recognized, all the journals have carried accounts—some of them highly exaggerated—of the attack and Mrs. Thynne's murderous attempt. Lady Sarn has suggested we advertise."

"I've no doubt you'll find them. Unfortunately, Mrs. Gantt's family is all too likely to try and take advantage of your unnecessary sense of guilt. Anna, you cannot blame yourself for that poor woman's death. It's damned arrogant. That she was killed instead of you was only a freak accident."

"I wonder. You may be right, Jesse. Perhaps I have been arrogant in assuming the blame."

chapter
XVI

Oliver's confidence and Jesse's subsequent interview with Anna had precisely the result the boy expected. There was no more talk of any early return to Norwood. So serious did Jesse consider the present situation that he allowed himself to be persuaded into a dreadful and terrible act—he bought a suit of formal dress clothes.

Jesse was thus most uncomfortably clad when next he saw Anna, at a ball given by Lady Webbe. Much though he despised the intricately tied cravat (the work of Oliver) and the binding jacket he wore, Jesse had to admit that the elegant designs considered de rigueur for evening parties suited Anna very well. She wore the rubies again, glowing brightly against the luminous clarity of her pale skin and the dark sheen of her hair. Her gown was simple and white, but in no way the youthful attire of the newly presented debutante. Mrs. Mattingly would have admired the way Anna's form had filled out with rest and good food. Many of the gentlemen certainly did.

Anna endured the admiring gentlemen politely, but without encouragement, and wished most heartily that Jesse would dispose of them all, rather than glaring at them from across the ballroom. Ever hopeful, she had saved the supper dance for Jesse. Being practical as well, Anna sent Lord Sarn to see that Jesse took it.

After Jesse had been giggled away from one corner by the debutantes, and glared away from another by the dowagers, he had taken a determined stand by the punch bowl, where his grim expression helped keep a group of high-spirited youths from adding a little extra spice to the refreshments. Lord Sarn joined his friend there, helped himself to a glass of champagne punch, and turned, with careful nonchalance, to watch the dancers.

"Very elegant turnout, Jess. If you'd only stop pulling at your cravat you'd look quite the Corinthian. It wouldn't hurt to cease looking at everyone as if you suspect them of cheating at cards either. And if your purpose is to frighten Anna's suitors away, it would be far more effective to go over there and dance with her yourself. Strangely enough, I do believe she has an empty space on her dance card. . . ."

Jesse looked sadly and directly into his friend's eyes. "Viv, in all the years we've known each other, have you ever seen me dance?"

"Oh. Oh. You fool! Why didn't you ask me to teach you? Or Oliver?"

"At my age? Don't be silly. If I've lived this long without learning to dance, I can do without it entirely." Just the same his eyes were envious as he watched the swirling couples. "Anna's very graceful, though, isn't she?"

"Yes. She was always very musical. Have you heard Anna's new wrinkle, by the way? Of course you have— that's why you're standing guard like this. You take it seriously then?"

"I always have. We were simply so involved in pursuing the jewels and Mrs. Thynne—the headmistress being the more immediate danger—that all the ramifications of Anna's story were not considered. Viv, don't try to tell me you think she was fantasizing again."

"I just don't know, Jess. Chloe believes Anna implicitly. Grandmama . . . has her doubts." The dowager thought Anna's claim was a very clever ploy to hook a certain recalcitrant bachelor, but Lord Sarn could hardly tell that to Jesse. "I respect Grandmama's opinion."

"And Chloe's? And mine, come to think of it?"

"You, sir, are prejudiced. And neither you nor my beloved have anything near Grandmama's years of experience. I tell you true, Jess, I don't know what to think. Part of me believes her. Part of me says there simply isn't anyone left to suspect. The idea that one of the villagers or one of Westerbrooke's guests will turn out to be a long-lost Gallant cousin is ridiculous. There's not one of them, village or visitor, whose ancestry isn't fully documented and publicly known for three centuries. If I absolutely have to believe in a second murderer, I'll plump for Anna's guardians."

"Anna says not."

"Her denial seems based more on personal opinion than fact. It's true the Rylands' allowance stopped with her death, but that doesn't mean they couldn't have other and stronger motives to wish Anna dead."

"Such as . . . ?"

"Lud, I don't know. But it certainly was convenient for them to declare Anna dead."

"True."

"Why don't you discuss my idea with Anna? Ask her to sit out the dance with you. The supper dance is right after. . . ."

"Where did she go? She was dancing with that toad Westerbrooke just a minute ago. I can't see them." Jesse interrupted his friend urgently.

"Really, Jess. Half the debs are togged out in white. How can you expect to pick out just one?"

"Where is Chloe?"

Sarn turned unerringly to the corner of the dance floor occupied by his fiancée. "There. With one of her brothers-in-law. Oh, I see what you mean. Well, someone probably trod on Anna's gown and she's gone to make repairs. Happens all the time."

"In that case the duke would hardly follow, and I don't see him about either."

"Surely you don't suspect the duke of . . . ?"

"Seduction? I do, and so would you if you'd seen him fawning over Anna—giving her books of poetry! He still wants to marry her!"

"There is no crime in that."

"Not if he pursues his course honorably and accepts his congé with dignity. His reputation, however, indicates that such gentlemanly behavior is not at all a matter of course. I'm going looking for them."

"Hold up, I'm coming with you. Dammit, Jess, calm down. If you make a fuss, you'll only hurt Anna."

Jesse's angry exit from the ballroom was certainly noted, but as most of London society considered his every move eccentric, this was merely taken as another example of provincial prudery. The promise of an exceptional buffet further distracted the guests, allowing Jesse to stalk down the hall, away from the ballroom, and peek into the rooms opening off it. It didn't take much searching to find Anna. Sounds of a scuffle could be heard from a few doors away.

The viscount was only a few steps behind Jesse, but even so, by the time he entered the small parlour and closed the door behind him Jesse had already grabbed the over-amorous duke by the collar of his elegant jacket and delivered a telling punch that left his grace dazed and flat on his back.

"Anna, are you all right?"

"I'll be fine." She smiled weakly. "Evidently I didn't handle him so well after all."

"What the hell got into you, Westerbrooke?" Sarn whispered vehemently. "I should think even you would know the difference between a ladybird and a lady."

The duke, returned to his senses, was horrified by his monumental lapse of decorum. "My lady, allow me to apologize most humbly for so allowing my passionate devotion to your sweet self to overcome my sense of propriety. The immoderate affection I entertain toward your ladyship must be—not my excuse, for there can be none—but the only-too-human explanation for my precipitate advances."

Jesse regarded with deep resentment the graceful way the duke rose from his ignominious position sprawled on Lady Webbe's fine oriental carpet. How dare he treat such criminal behavior as if it were a minor social faux pas on his part! A grim smile made the duke sidestep very carefully, avoiding the irate Mr. Norwood, to throw himself on his knees before Anna.

"I had not meant to speak so soon, Lady Annabelle, but the force of my emotions can no longer be contained. What was once arranged for us as a convenient and suitable alliance has become the dearest wish of my heart. Although I have been silent until this moment, I think my unspoken affection has been easily discerned by your clear-sighted gaze. Fear for your safety bids me put my fate to the test without delay. Lady Annabelle, beloved, will you do me the inestimable honor of becoming my duchess?"

"Really, Westerbrooke, this is hardly the time or the place!" exclaimed Lord Sarn with exasperation. He was keeping an anxious eye on the doorway, and an even more anxious one on his enraged friend.

"Haven't you insulted Lady Annabelle enough for one evening? I suggest you find your way home before the guests notice you're sporting a black eye—and before you earn another one," Jesse threatened.

"My lady, I appeal to you. I do not deserve such brusque treatment. And I do deserve an answer."

Anna forestalled another outburst by her champion with her swift reply. "Yes, your grace, you do deserve a direct answer. I am afraid that that answer is not, and can never be, such as you desire. The peculiar circumstances of my unhappy past have left me most unsuited for the position your wife would occupy in the world. And while my sentiments for you are all that is kind and full of respect for your position, they are not those I should hope to feel for a prospective husband. Nor can I give you any hope that my sentiments will change with time. I am sorry that you should be given my refusal so publicly, but, remember, it was you who insisted on making your offer before an audience. I need hardly assure you that Lord Sarn and Mr. Norwood will remain as silent as I regarding your confidences this evening."

The duke rose from his knees stiffly, unbelieving. His

hands were clenched tightly to control his disappointment. Almost automatically he took a single step toward Anna, as if to plead for a single word that would offer the very hope her earlier words so clearly denied.

Distrustful of the duke's reaction, Jesse too took a step forward. Before his closed fist could reach its destination, luckily, the door opened to admit the dowager Lady Sarn and the prospective Lady Sarn, Chloe.

"Anna, what are you doing in here? Everybody is at supper. You're a prize catch, your hostess is bound to notice your absence." The old lady's piercing gaze swept the room. "Misbehaving? Having a dust-up? Very bad form, boys. Do something with your cravat, Westerbrooke. You don't have to advertise your folly to the rest of the world."

The duke had hardly rearranged the folds of his cravat to his satisfaction, when the proof of the dowager's words was brought home. Lady Webbe had scored quite a coup in bringing the heiress to her ball and she did not mean to let Anna disappear before the maximum number of guests were aware of her success. Now that Jesse was unlikely to dismember the duke without further ado, and Anna was properly chaperoned once more, Lord Sarn had relaxed his vigilance at the doorway. Lady Webbe was thus able to push her smiling way into the tense group, followed by some of the more inquisitive of her guests, including none other than Lady Jersey. The scent of scandal was in the air.

"My dear Lady Annabelle, whatever are you doing here? If you are not feeling quite the thing, I can send for Sir Henry Halford for you."

"Dear Lady Webbe, it is I who must apologize, I and my graceless grandson." The dowager took her hostess firmly by the arm and began leading her in the direction of the door again. "Sarn had some news of that unfortunate woman who was killed in the attack on Lady Annabelle's coach and nothing would do but he must gather us all together to tell us at once. Such an impatient boy."

"It seemed so convenient," Sarn answered apologetically, quickly taking the dowager's lead. "All of us here together. But I never intended disrupting your festivities, Lady Webbe.''

"So you've found the woman's family. How interesting,'' commented Lady Webbe in depressing tones.

"Well, no, actually we haven't been able to discover a thing. But what's happened that's truly fascinating is that someone else is on the same trail. Everywhere my agent goes in his search he finds the same two men have been before him! Don't you think that's interesting?''

The duke, his face pale and beaded with perspiration, added his part to the charade in a strained voice. "I'm afraid that's no mystery, Sarn, old boy. If you'd only told me before what you meant to do, I could have saved you the trouble. I've had some of my men trying to discover the lady's family ever since Lady Annabelle's claim was brought forward. After all, the woman is buried in my family chapel.''

"So much for your big news, milord,'' his hostess said waspishly. "Will you return to the ballroom now?''

In the general exeunt from the parlour, Lady Jersey latched herself on to the duke with a wicked smile on her lips and a determined clasp on his arm. For once in her life the notorious gossip must have been unsuccessful, however, for the next day she proclaimed that contact with the straitlaced Sarns and other provincials (by which she meant Jesse) had quite spoiled the duke's rakish charm. She added nastily that as the tactic seemed to have had no effect on the heiress for whom the display of virtue was intended, Westerbrooke might as well desist and return to the behavior that had long proved successful with the ladies.

chapter
XVII

Jesse and Lord Sarn had a few things to say about the duke as well when they met the next day at Boodles. In comparison, Lady Jersey's remarks were charitable.

"I wish he weren't a neighbor," Lord Sarn said. "You, of course, won't mind cutting him dead, but it will be awkward for me. We serve on a number of committees together."

"You won't be the first member of county society to take to avoiding Westerbrooke."

"Oh yes, your brother. Another woman, wasn't it?"

"What else? At the time I suspected my brother to have been equally at fault. Now I wonder."

"For a man with a reputation as a successful rake, the duke behaved with an astounding lack of subtlety."

"Didn't he though?"

"What do you mean by that?" Sarn asked.

"I mean only a fool could possibly find encouragement in Anna's words or actions for that sort of behavior. Only a fool could expect her to respond other than she did. And Westerbrooke, for all his faults, is not a fool."

"But that's dastardly. You think he did it on purpose."

"I already warned Anna that I thought the duke capable of trying to frighten her into marrying him. Just think what would have happened if we hadn't reached the room before Lady Webbe and Lady Jersey. What if Anna had become so frightened she screamed for help? The fact that she was the duke's victim wouldn't have mattered in the least. Ruin or marriage would have been the choice.''

"Anna would choose ruin first."

"Yes, we know that, but Westerbrooke wouldn't. Anna fought too hard for her position to forfeit it lightly. And the duke would have been quick to remind her that once she married she would be free from any danger from long-lost heirs. Then no doubt he would have paraded his wounded heart before her. Even he must see how hungry for affection Anna is. Oh yes, it would seem like quite a good plan to him.''

"But why? For all his vaunted affection, the duke doesn't really care that much for Anna. I don't think he knows how."

"I can only assume that the duke's title cost him more than he could easily afford. In short, nothing less than the combined Gallant fortunes will satisfy his needs.''

"Impossible! The fortune he inherited was fabulous!''

"To us, surely. But we do not play whist with the Duke of York for five guineas a point. Nor do we generously loan large sums to the Prince of Wales which will never be recovered.''

"The swine! Well, just let a hint of financial difficulties get around, and Westerbrooke may find he's not society's darling anymore.''

Jesse smiled, his humor restored at the thought of the duke despised, exiled. "Unfortunately, if his pockets are to let and he is forced to rusticate, we'll be forced to endure his company in the country.''

"Yes, but if he's known to be ruined, we can all cut him with a clear conscience.''

"I'm just thankful Anna doesn't have to put up with his encroaching manners anymore. He'll not dare to come sneaking back after last night's fiasco.''

Anna had some qualms about meeting the duke alone after the distressing occurrence of the previous evening, but she sensed Westerbrooke would not be satisfied until he had tried once more to atone and to woo, and she preferred to get it over with once and for all. Due to the immediate and threatening presence of Jesse Norwood, Anna had been unable to give the duke her most decisive reason for refusing his offer last night. She would do so now. And if she wished most heartily that Lady Sarn had not chosen this particular afternoon to visit an ailing friend, Anna consoled herself with the knowledge that there were three strong footmen and a haughty butler nearby who would come to her rescue at the first sign of trouble.

In order to depress his pretensions thoroughly, Anna made quite sure the interview with Westerbrooke would be conducted as formally as possible. She wore a severely cut walking gown to better hint that her time was valuable and the duke was delaying her planned activities. Her back was ramrod straight and her expression was one the royal house of Zschau reserved for impertinent upstarts.

The formal drawing room was her choice of setting for what would no doubt be a most difficult conversation. Of all the rooms in Lady Sarn's town house this was the least used, the least marked by the dowager's vibrant personality.

Anna had trifled with the idea of returning to the duke all the small tokens he had pressed upon her in the last few weeks. They were hardly the sort of things she would keep and treasure in any case, being the obvious choices of one who knew only the superficial tastes of the recipient. The book of poetry was a good example. Anna loved poetry, loved the way good verse tasted when read aloud, loved the way it gave wing to the imagination. What Westerbrooke had given her was a collection of doggerel. The excessively florid dedication to Edward, first Duke of Westerbrooke, Marquess of Alder, Viscount of Gantt, Baron Rowe of Rowely, etc., as patron only emphasized the man's complete lack of any real aesthetic appreciation. To return the gifts, however, would be to give them an importance they did not merit, imputing a relationship less than casual. It would also have been an unnecessary slap in the face.

The duke was too properly abject for such rudeness. Like a child who has been caught in some mischief, Westerbrooke approached abashed, repentant, and fearful of punishment.

"Lady Annabelle, how kind and gracious of you to see me again after my disgraceful behavior yesternight. I cannot tell you how much I appreciate this generosity on your part."

Anna raised a single eyebrow in an intimidating manner. "Then I suggest you do not try. I must confess, your grace, that I only agreed to see you again in order to assure you beyond any question of doubt that I meant every word I spoke last night."

"I feared it. My folly, my uncontrollable passion, have given you a lasting disgust of me. But no, you are the soul of justice. You would never condemn a man for a single lapse. Another chance is all I ask, another chance to prove my worth, to win your forgiveness . . . to win your heart."

"My forgiveness I give you freely." Though Anna tried to deny the thought, there was a part of her that felt guilty that she had not seen last night's embrace coming, had not known how to deflect it.

Unfortunately, this slight condescension sent the duke into a frenzy of joy. He fell to his knees and pressed a kiss, carefully chaste, upon Anna's reluctant hand. "Too good, too generous woman. I knew you could not remain cold to the pleas of a devoted heart. Soon, soon you will see how worthy of your trust I am."

"Not if you continue to indulge in theatrics such as these, your grace. Pray rise and calm yourself."

"Ah, my lady, it is so hard to mask the depth of my feelings. These feelings are too new, too strong. I have not yet learned to handle them."

"Such behavior hardly bodes well for your promises for the future. But, as I said last night, I can give you no hope for that future. No, let me speak. First, my refusal of your offer was in no way the result of anger at your foolishness, but the result of careful consideration. Our tastes and habits of mind are too different for us ever to enjoy the comfortable companionship that should be present in a marriage."

"Ah, say not so."

"Hear me out. There are other considerations as well. You have told me often that you feel my only lasting safety is in marriage. Whether this is true or not, I could never wed for such a reason. More than that, until the mystery of who attacked my carriage is completely resolved, I can make no plans for the future. That part of my life must be completed before I can move on."

"You're wrong, you know." The duke was fighting to remain calm. "You must put that part of your life aside, forget it entirely, in order to get on with living. Finding the murderers has become an obsession with you. But it's not your responsibility. Leave it to the law."

"The law? The law thinks the murderers are all either captured or dead. I'm not sure even Lord Sarn believes me, believes that I saw two men who have not been accounted for. He thinks I was hallucinating."

"Can you honestly say that is impossible? You were near death. Stripped, buried in the snow, a bullet through your shoulder—is it any wonder if your memory is confused?"

"I saw the murderers before I was shot," Anna reminded the duke mulishly. She was becoming annoyed at having her word distrusted.

"You saw—what? Through a blizzard? Men who were muffled up to their ears. They had pistols pointed at you, yet what you noticed was the color of their eyes, the sound of their voices. Look, I'll cover my face. Could you recognize me? My voice?"

Anna shivered and turned pale.

"Forgive me, my lady." The duke was instantly contrite. "It's only that I cannot bear to see you torture yourself by holding on to the past. It is time to let go."

"I cannot. An innocent woman died. Until her family is found, until her affairs are settled, her murder avenged, my plans must be held in abeyance."

"You cannot hold yourself responsible for that woman's death, Lady Annabelle! Blame two greedy men with guns, blame fate, but not yourself."

"I don't blame myself for her death, not anymore. But

she seemed in many ways a kindred spirit, lonely and afraid. She does not deserve to have her passing go unnoticed, unmourned. She left a child."

"That . . . that's very sad, but. . . ."

"Who does not even know his mother is dead."

"But you don't need to concern yourself with that. Naturally, I have been trying diligently to discover this woman's next of kin. Leave it to me," the duke insisted. "It's time you began to live again. Stop wasting your life agonizing over a silly peagoose who had nothing to recommend her but a pair of sparkling blue eyes and a dimple when she smiled. She wasn't worth your notice alive; she's not worth it dead."

Jesse shook his head in disgust. He had been persuaded to visit the club only in order to seek the latest news from the Continent. The threat of invasion was still a very present fear, and he wanted to pick up as much news as he could. For every piece of real information he gathered, however, there was also a piece of gossip, which more often than not included the name of Lady Annabelle Gallant. Oh, nothing scandalous, of course. Speculation as to the extent of her fortune. Odds on the betting books as to the favorite among her suitors . . .

"Shall we?" Sarn teased his scowling friend. "We could make a fortune betting against the duke's chances before anyone else realizes he's been given the boot."

"I don't find that amusing, Viv."

"Don't get on your high ropes. No one means any disrespect to Anna by it."

"No one means her any good either. Anna told me Westerbrooke was not at all the worst of her suitors, but I didn't appreciate the full magnitude of the situation before. I don't know how it is that such a serene woman can engender such disquiet, but she leaves me in a constant state of anxiety. She really shouldn't be left at large without a keeper. If she's not in danger from greedy murderers, then she must ward off greedy seducers. And once she gets a bee in her bonnet about something, we're all doomed. She won't rest until she's accomplished all she meant to do. Like finding the attackers of her coach.''

"And finding the family of that poor woman who died. I know what you mean. That reminds me, I promised to give her a report from the agent I had working on that.'' Sarn felt in his waistcoat pocket to make sure he still carried the information.

"Oh, then there really was a report. At the time I thought you'd invented it to distract the gossip-mongers.''

"No, I'm not that clever. Here it is. I scanned it only briefly myself. For a moment I thought we might have had something with this story of someone else trying to track down Mrs. Gantt's background, but Westerbrooke put an end to that idea.''

"I'm surprised Westerbrooke went to such trouble. Your man certainly has been thorough, according to this report. Strange that this woman's background should be so elusive.''

"Oh, I don't know. . . .''

Suddenly Jesse bolted out of his chair. "My God, Viv, did you see this?''

An ancient club member glared at him pointedly.

"Well, if you will stop waving it under my nose I may be able to see which part you mean.''

"'One strange circumstance has recurred repeatedly in my investigations,''' Jesse quoted.

"About the two men who preceded him on the same errand. I told you about that.''

"But the description, man, the description! 'Every person I questioned told the same story. I was not the first to ask these questions. Two, by their descriptions always the same two, had gone before me on the same quest—the spokesman, a countryman with some little education, tall, fair with eyes of a strange, tawny gold color; the other a small, nervous type with dark eyes and hair. A few have commented that this second man seemed not quite normal.'''

"I don't quite. . . . Is it possible? Then . . . then there are four men trying to trace Mrs. Gantt—the duke's men . . . and the murderers.''

"Or the duke's men are the murderers.''

The next minute Lord Sarn was chasing Jesse from the reading room and out of the club onto St. James Street.

"Jesse, wait up. Jess! Jess, it doesn't make sense. Why would the duke want to kill Anna?"

"Not Anna, never Anna. No wonder it didn't make sense before. Mrs. Gantt was the intended victim."

"That doesn't make sense either. Why would the duke want to kill her?" Lord Sarn was out of breath and confused.

"I don't know, but considering his reputation, I can hazard a guess."

"Just tell me one more thing. Where are we rushing off to?"

"To Anna. I know it's not reasonable. There's no reason to think she could be in any danger. She's safe at home with Lady Sarn. I know all that. But just the same. . . ."

"Actually, I believe Grandmama is out visiting an old crony of hers." The two men exchanged glances full of uneasiness.

"A hackney!"

"No, not fast enough. Look, here's Alvanly—driving his grays. Just the thing."

Anna repeated the duke's words slowly, as if in shock. "A silly peagoose who had nothing to recommend her but a pair of sparkling blue eyes and a dimple when she smiled."

"Forgive me, Lady Annabelle. I shouldn't have said that. The strength of my emotion leads me to speak with more force than is perhaps seemly."

"No, you should not have said that," Anna responded in a faint voice. Images crowded in her mind—the beautiful face of poor, troubled Annabelle Gantt, the inscription on a gold wedding band, the pompous dedication of a bad poet, and the dowager's cynical evaluation of the duke's bad—and good—points. "I never saw her smile, you know."

"What? I don't understand."

"I never saw her dimples."

"An example only." Westerbrooke became flustered. "An image of a beautiful and brainless woman."

"Why should you assume her brainless? I never said so. You knew her."

"I? Don't be ridiculous."

"You were the first murderer. I was not the intended victim after all. It was Mrs. Gantt."

"Lady Annabelle, you need not fling mad accusations at me in order to drive me from your side. These insults are poor return for genuine, if unrequited, devotion. You know perfectly well that my entire household and any number of guests can swear to my whereabouts the evening of the attack. Let me add that should you be so malicious as to repeat these slanders, I will not be slow in taking legal action."

"Eventually proof of your marriage will be found. 'May 3, 1801 Love, Edward.' I suppose the ring is what your men were searching so diligently for. Of course, you have an alibi for the night of the murder. You would never have the courage to act yourself. But the man you sent shared the distinctive family eyes—your bastard half brother?"

This last was only a guess on Anna's part, but by the duke's frightened reaction, an inspired one.

"No, no, it's not true," Westerbrooke denied, panicking.

"You must think me a fool as well. Only a rogue and blackmailer could have persuaded my aunt and uncle to permit my marriage. The idea that a man of your years could be a passive partner in all those arrangements defies belief. From the first I was aware you were only interested in my wealth. At the time your greed was a mark in your favor, but now I see the truth, Edward Arthur Rowe, Duke of Westerbrooke, Marquess of Alder, Viscount of *Gantt*."

"A coincidence only. It is not that uncommon a name."

"There are too many coincidences, your grace. Why do you look so pale if my deductions are false? The truth or falseness of my words can easily be confirmed. You may have used another name when you married the girl, but your signature will be recognizable, your face too if the vicar is still alive. Then there's your half brother. How far can you trust him—and his unsteady companion?"

"Bert won't betray me. And neither will you, my dear

Lady Annabelle. Once we're married, you'll find it much more convenient to stay quiet."

"You cannot force me to marry you."

"Haven't you learned anything from your sojourn with Mrs. Thynne? I got a special license for our arranged marriage and I've kept it with me ever since your claim was proved. There are men in some parts of this city who don't give a damn whether the bride says yea or nay, so long as they are paid enough."

Anna remained unperturbed. She shook her head sadly. "Not entirely trusting you to behave as a gentleman should, I took the precaution of requesting the footmen to hover in the vicinity. You cannot hope to overpower everyone you meet from Grosvenor Square to the rookeries."

"This pistol . . ." He pulled the weapon from his waistcoat. ". . . should guarantee the compliance of your servants."

"But not mine. You can't do it, Westerbrooke. With all the gossips on this Square, do you think your entrance was not noted? Do you think you can drag me from here—kicking and screaming, or unconscious—without every tongue for miles wagging with the news of it? It's over, your grace."

Jesse and Lord Sarn, entering silently behind the duke, pulled swords from a decorative arrangement on the wall. Then quietly they stepped forward and pointed them at the murderer's neck.

"It's over, your grace," Jesse reiterated.

chapter
XVIII

In the end it was not the murder of his wife, but the attempted disinheritance of his son that spelled the death sentence for Edward, Duke of Westerbrooke. The existence of a child was the one secret he had kept from his half brother. Bert was loyal to the sibling who had done so much for him as long as he believed he was only eliminating a conniving mistress. Condemning an innocent child to bastardy was the one crime the illegitimate Bert would neither perform nor condone. Captured and brought face to face with his legitimate half brother, Bert committed his last crime and delivered the duke up to a higher court of justice.

"I cannot believe the authorities were so lax as to leave the man with a weapon. Didn't they search him?" Lady Sarn asked the company in general.

The gathering at her town house was not one that London society would have called fashionable, but it was a great deal more enjoyable. Due to the large number of guests, the conclave was being held in the very room where Anna and the duke had held their final confrontation. All traces of formality had disappeared from the drawing room, however. No unhappy memories were allowed to cling to the place. Freed from fear and her obligation to the deceased Annabelle, Anna had regained the serenity that was hers by nature.

Only one circumstance marred her happiness—Jesse was not there.

"Oh, they searched him," Sarn answered when a pointed finger in his ribs finally gained his attention. "But they neglected to check his boots. He was bound as well, so the officials cannot be blamed for thinking him rendered harmless."

"I can blame them. Although I suppose it's all for the best. Think what a scandal it would have made."

"Remarkable, isn't it?" Anna commented. "That a man should be so ruthless a villain, and still possess such scruples. Bert has made a complete confession as to his and his cohort's part in the attack. But he refuses to implicate the duke and claims that murder was due to long-standing disagreements. I can only think this reticence is due to concern for the child, that the boy should not grow up with the knowledge that his father had had his mother killed."

"A much cleaner solution," said the dowager with satisfaction.

"And the child?" Chloe asked.

"Well cared for," Anna told her. "We finally found the family Annabelle had left when she ran off with Westerbrooke. They're good, kind people who've been terribly distressed at the loss of their daughter."

"The father of 'Mrs. Gantt,' as she thought herself, is a country vicar," Sarn explained. "His wife, Annabelle's mother, is no longer living, but there are still three daughters and two sons at home."

"I'm glad," said Chloe. "But I'm not sure I understand the whole sequence of events yet. If the duke knew where his wife's family were, what were the two men searching for? And which villainy was the duke's and which Mrs. Thynne's?"

"Yes, tell us, Anna. I've been trying to reconcile what we've discovered with your original story of the attack, but I'm not sure I have all the pieces of the puzzle," Oliver added his plea.

"I suppose most of the confusion stemmed from the bizarre coincidence that placed 'Mrs. Gantt' and me in the same coach. That and our absolute certainty that greed for my money was at the bottom of the attack. As I suppose it was, in a way.

"Annabelle Gantt's tragedy began four years ago when she met the duke. With her proper vicarage upbringing she was one girl the duke couldn't seduce. Being unable to accept defeat, he married her. But he had enough native caution to use another name—one of his lesser titles. I should have caught that sooner—Herries was one of my grandfather's lesser titles.

"Anyway, Westerbrooke probably never considered this a 'real' marriage, however legal it was. Eventually he tired of Annabelle. And his finances grew worse. His title cost more dearly than anyone guessed. A rich wife was an immediate necessity. Fate gave him the ammunition to blackmail my aunt and uncle into arranging a marriage with me. But his legal right to my fortune would be exploded if his first marriage came to light—and that was something he dared not risk."

"So, he planned to murder his wife," said Oliver.

"Actually, I don't think that was his first thought. When he was taken, Westerbrooke tried to explain. His original plan was simply to destroy the evidence of the marriage. Without proof, Annabelle would simply be viewed as a vengeful mistress. The parson who performed the ceremony, however, could not be bribed. And Annabelle, grown suspicious, put her child and her marriage lines out of reach. At some time Westerbrooke must have let slip the general area of his home. Annabelle decided to discover the secret behind the duke's life away from her. And he decided at last that she would have to die."

"Yes, I'm afraid she was doomed from the day Westerbrooke married her. Sooner or later he was going to have to look around for a rich, well-born bribe. If not me, someone else."

"Come on, gel. Get on with it."

"Yes, my lady. As the date of our wedding approached, Westerbrooke had to act fast. He spun some elaborate tale to his half brother and sent Bert to dispose of his wife. Bert must have been following the duke's wife all along, but the right opportunity to attack didn't come until we had almost arrived.''

"Bert and his cohort were the original pair who stopped your coach," prodded Oliver.

"Right. Westerbrooke had assumed that his wife would be carrying her marriage lines on her, since he knew she'd removed them from their house. That—and her wedding ring—is what they were searching for all along. Meanwhile, Mrs. Thynne's lackeys were waiting to dispose of me and remove any identification I might have carried. I think they must have scared Bert and his friend away. They came upon the scene to find their job already done for them. So they contented themselves with doing a very sloppy job of burying the bodies and gathering up the scattered luggage the first pair of villains left behind. The blizzard had grown worse by the minute, however, and not knowing the area well, Mrs. Thynne's hired killers became irrevocably lost and died of exposure.''

"But the duke's men simply returned home. And with all the visiting guests, a few more horses in the stable wouldn't be noticed!" Oliver said.

Lord Sarn put his head in his hands. "Do you know, Jesse suggested that very thing the night the Rylands were murdered. But we never imagined. . . ."

"Westerbrooke must have gone into a terrible panic when it seemed his plan had backfired and he'd killed the wrong bride." The dowager laughed.

"Lord, yes," her grandson agreed. "No wonder his grief seemed genuine. He didn't just make up that story about the letters to look good. He needed an excuse to cover up the fact that he had overreacted."

"Then I forced Anna's identity into the open, and he thought he had another chance," added Chloe.

"What I want to know," interrupted the doctor, who had been listening quietly until that moment, "is first, why did your aunt and uncle identify Mrs. Gantt's body as yours?"

"Well, I'm only guessing, mind, but I think it was the only way to get away from all their blackmailers—not only the duke, but Mrs. Thynne. They were about to lose my money anyway if I married the duke, but the blackmailing would never stop so long as I lived."

"But if you turned up alive later?"

"They could either deny me, or say they'd made a mistake. My aunt and uncle didn't think very far ahead."

"Yes, that sounds like something those fools would do," Doctor Abernathy agreed. "The other thing I want to know is what tipped you off to the duke? You hadn't seen the report."

"I never trusted him. And those eyes bothered me. But when he was talking to me, he made a bad slip. He described Annabelle as a 'silly peagoose who had nothing to recommend her but a pair of sparkling blue eyes and a dimple when she smiled.' Now I had never mentioned a dimple. She hadn't smiled, so I had never seen it. But he had. Suddenly it all came together. I'd just been looking at that stupid book he gave me—the one with the silly dedication that listed all his titles. And I remembered what Lady Sarn had once said about his interest in his bastard relatives."

"Well, I think you were inspired," cried Oliver. "No matter what Jesse says."

"You needn't tell me what that is. Jesse thinks only a brainless idiot would have opened her mouth and voiced her suspicions to a probable murderer. I have to confess he has a point."

Later, in the flurry of good-byes, Anna found a moment to pull Oliver aside and question him.

"Why wouldn't he come, Noll?"

"Lord, I don't know, Anna. Afraid to see you again, I suppose. He's acting like a fool. He's packed and unpacked four times during the last week. But he is going to leave."

"Without saying good-bye?"

The youth shrugged, helplessly. "Anna couldn't you . . . give up the money?"

"Could you give up Norwood?"

"Norwood? But that's my . . . my . . ."

"Your heritage? Well, this is mine. Great wealth is also a great responsibility. I can't simply hand it over to someone else and trust that he will use it properly."

"I'm sorry. I understand. It's just. . . ."

"I know, Noll, I know."

At the ungodly hour of six the next morning, Jesse Norwood appeared, ready for travel, at the doorstep of the Sarn household, where he caused no end of a stir. The tweeny who had timidly answered the door, an action that was not properly her province at all, was so flustered at seeing a member of the upper class awake, dressed, and calling at an hour when most of London society had just retired, that she was unable to answer the gentleman intelligibly at all. Even Lady Sarn's very correct butler was guilty of a raised eyebrow. His voice was coolly patient as he stated the obvious.

"His lordship is still abed. Would the matter be urgent, Mr. Norwood?"

"Not urgent, no. I just wanted to pop up and say. . . ."

Jesse's intentions were interrupted by the appearance of yet another member of the aristocracy to whom early hours presented no terrors.

"I think we'll leave Lord Sarn's rest undisturbed for a little while longer." Anna's voice boded no good for someone. "Were you going to leave without saying good-bye?"

"I wrote a letter."

"Coward."

"Yes. You're not going to make this easy for me, are you?"

"I intend to make it as difficult as I possibly can."

"Then perhaps we had better find someplace less public to speak. Soames, would you ask my coachman to walk the horses. Evidently I'll be a little longer than I expected."

"Yes, sir. There's a fire in the library, sir."

The corner by the library fire was obviously one of Anna's favorite nooks. Her shawl was draped over the back of a comfortable wing chair, a book of poems by Wordsworth rested on a table by the side. Some of her correspondence, invitations and a partially written letter, marked the place where she had put the book down. Jesse remembered the small changes Anna had wrought at Norwood, the way her presence had permeated the house. He wondered how he was going to survive the desperate loneliness of his life without Anna. But he remained determined.

"I had hoped that you would understand, Anna. We've accomplished all we meant to do—you've been restored to your rightful position, and the murderers have all been brought to justice. It has given me a great deal of satisfaction and pleasure to see you living the sort of life to which you were born, moving among the first circles of society, wealthy and assured. But this is not my world! Can't you see I don't belong here?"

Anna took a deep breath and tried to speak calmly and reasonably. She was frightened for her life now just as surely as she had been when she escaped Mrs. Thynne's clutches. This was too important to her.

"I think it is you who do not understand, Jesse. Of course you don't belong here. You've endured all this patiently, but you've not been comfortable. You've far too much ability and energy to tolerate idleness for long. And you are far too honest for society to feel very comfortable with you. Although you have come a long way from the hermit's life you led when we met, you could never endure the long succession of parties, routs, drums, and soirées, night after night, given by people one barely knows. I do realize all that."

"Then let me go, Anna."

"I'm not trying to hold you to a way of life you dislike. I am trying to make you see that I no more belong in the world I have described than you do. Haven't you learned by now that all your preconceived notions of the society heiress have nothing to do with reality? And that mere possession of a large fortune cannot turn me into that conventional picture you have in your head?"

Jesse carefully kept his distance.

"I never thought you could be conventional in any way. But if your wealth does not place you in that fashionable world, your birth, your early upbringing do. You told us yourself how happy your childhood days were, those days when you played in the royal courts of Europe and the King of France gave you presents. You've used the word 'heritage' often in the quest to regain your name and fortune. Well, that is your heritage.''

"Those days were happy," Anna conceded. "But they were happy because I was loved and cared for and protected by my parents and my mother's family at Zschau. It was not the money, or our position in society that made ours a loving and contented home. And neither the money nor society can re-create that world.''

"You'll find the affection you hope for. Anyone who truly knew you must come to care for you,'' Jesse said with difficulty. "But I think that because of the misery and loneliness of the last years of your imprisonment, you still need time to find your balance, to put your feelings of gratitude into proper perspective.''

"You're being terribly insulting, Jesse. I had not thought that you considered me just another woolly-headed female.''

"I don't!''

"Then give me the credit for knowing my own mind—and heart. Don't you see? Those long solitary years have left me unfit for the kind of fashionable life to which you mean to condemn me. I know too much of the darker side of humanity to concentrate my energies on the latest gossip or a new bonnet. I still have a great capacity for joy, but not for frivolity.''

"Sarn's not frivolous, yet he enjoys the *ton*.''

"In small doses and never taken too seriously. His heart isn't here, and neither is mine. I think you know where my heart is.''

Jesse retreated another step behind the chair. The look in Anna's eyes filled him with misgivings. "Anna, I just want you to have the best.''

She smiled blindingly, full of confidence. Boldly she closed the distance between them and put her arms around Jesse's neck and kissed him.

"You are the best.''

"Anna. . . .''

"No, listen to me. For almost all of my life, my fortune

has stood between me and happiness. Are you going to let it happen again? Will you leave me to the fortune hunters?''

Against his will, Jesse's arms had reached out to hold Anna against his chest, to caress lightly her shiny curls. ''Hussy. Do I make you happy?''

Anna nodded, smiling, into his shoulder. She knew she'd won. ''I don't know why it is, so very disagreeable as you are, but I really don't think I can ever be happy without you.''

''You could have anyone. . . .''

''Like Westerbrooke? Thank you, no. I don't want anyone, I want you. Would anyone else risk his life for me? Would anyone else care for me as you did—while you still believed me a poor governess?''

Jesse muttered unintelligibly into her hair for a moment. ''Are you sure, Anna?''

''Do you love me?''

''Have you brazenly thrown yourself at me without being sure?'' he teased. Then he answered very seriously, ''Yes, I love you. By heaven, how I love you!''

Jesse silently threw in the towel and proceeded to show Anna just how much he loved her.

They were still enjoyably occupied in a mutual demonstration of affection when Oliver burst in, full of news. So distracted was the youth that it took him a minute before he quite assimilated the tableau before him.

''Anna, Anna, he's gone. When I got up this morning his room was empty and one of the coaches was. . . . Oh. Oh!''

''I didn't get very far,'' explained Jesse, without, however, releasing his captive.

''I say, does this mean . . . are you betrothed?''

''Now that I think of it, a formal offer has not been made,'' said Anna, unperturbed.

''No? I thought you had proposed. In any case, I accept.'' Joy had made Jesse light-headed as well as lighthearted.

''I think that's good enough to hold up in a court of law. In any case I could always say I'd found you in . . . in *flagrante delicto*. And then he'd have to marry you, Anna.''

''While I am, of course, overjoyed to discover that some

remnants of Latin still cling to your brain, I do think your time might be better employed right now. For example, you might find the coachman and send him home."

"Ummm? Oh, yes." Oliver started out, but at the door he changed his mind and ran back to give Anna a chaste salute. "I'm so glad."

"Oliver," urged his uncle.

"I'm going. I say, have you realized? Anna is going to be my aunt!"

"Dreadful thought. Now go, boy."

The door closed for a second, then reopened just a crack. "May I tell the others?"

"Not for another half hour. Now. . . ."

"I'm gone."

"Now, where was I?" Anna helped him find his place.

"You know, for a recently reformed misogynist you seem awfully good at this."

"For someone who spent the last thirteen years in a young ladies seminary you're remarkably adept yourself. I didn't have a chance, did I?"

Anna did not pretend to misunderstand him. "Did you think I would let you go without a fight?"

"I should have remembered that you never give up. At one time it seemed an admirable quality."

"I intend to make you glad of it again."

"Then do so. And hush. We've only half an hour."

"We've the rest of our lives." But she hushed just the same.